Praise for *Sabbath of the Fox-Devils*

"Light the black candles and invert the cross as Sam Richard conjures a coming-of-age story of Satanic panic, creature carnage, and blasphemous terror!"

— Ryan Harding (*Genital Grinder*, *Header 3*)

"It's been said good writing comes from opening a vein and bleeding on the page. Anyone who's read Sam Richard knows his writing epitomizes this visceral process. *Sabbath of the Fox Devils*, both a wistful love letter to schlocky horror and a sentimental character study, is no different. It's a confidently-written, refined novella without sacrificing the rawness which made Sam's previous works so memorable. Fans of 80s horror, Scooby Doo, and punk rock will find lots to love here."

— Lucas Mangum, author of *Saint Sadist* & *Gods of the Dark Web*

"*Sabbath of the Fox-Devils* is coming-of-age gone wrong, a celebration of the Satan-soaked stories that hooked us all on horror and a satire of the people who hate them. I bet my soul you'll enjoy it as much as I did."

— KATY MICHELLE QUINN, AUTHOR OF *WINNIE*

Praise for *To Wallow in Ash & Other Sorrows*

"A punch to the soul. I mean you can really feel how difficult this was to write. *To Wallow in Ash & Other Sorrows* is a bleakly profound - and on occasion uplifting - expedition through grief-induced mania (and without ever succumbing to mal du siècle). Richard offers us an authentic, raw document of depression and loss; and to have moulded the stages into artful monographs while staring the abyss right in the eye every step of the way is truly commendable."

— CHRIS KELSO, AUTHOR OF *THE BLACK DOG EATS THE CITY*

"This book is grief weaponized."

— EMMA ALICE JOHNSON, WONDERLAND BOOK AWARD-WINNER

"Witches and rituals and weird gods but most terrifying of all is a sense of deep grief that stalks the pages like a predatory beast. Sam Richard has gifted readers his private terrors but also his heart and soul. Violent, weird, and compelling work."

— Nicholas Day, This Is Horror and Wonderland Award-nominated author of *At the End of the Day I Burst into Flames* and *Now That We're Alone*

"With *To Wallow in Ash & Other Sorrows*, Sam Richard has crafted a book of stories that will rip your heart right out of your chest... and it's absolutely worth every moment. At turns brutally raw, incredibly beautiful, and always unexpected, this is an unforgettable ode to a love lost far too soon, and a collection that is absolutely worth seeking out."

— Gwendolyn Kiste, author of *The Rust Maidens* and *The Invention of Ghosts*

✝

SABBATH OF THE FOX-DEVILS

SAM RICHARD

+

Copyright © 2020 Authors, Artists, Weirdpunk Books

First Edition

WP-0007

Front cover art and design by Michael Bukowski and lastchanceillustration.wordpress.com

Back cover/spine layout and formatting by Don Noble

Internal layout and formatting by Sam Richard

Photo of the author and his late-wife courtesy of Carla Rodriguez of Blkk Hand

Weirdpunk Books logo by Nate Sorenson

Weirdpunk Books

www.weirdpunkbooks.com

CONTENTS

Chapter 1   11
Chapter 2   19
Chapter 3   27
Chapter 4   41
Chapter 5   61
Chapter 6   69
Chapter 7   79
Chapter 8   87
Chapter 9   97
Chapter 10   105
Chapter 11   115
Chapter 12   123
Chapter 13   135
Chapter 14   141

Afterword   147
Acknowledgments   151
About the Author   153
Also by Weirdpunk Books   155

CHAPTER 1

I beg you, take this guilt, God. Release me from this suffering and shame. Ease my burden. Down on bended knee, I submit to you oh Lord. That was the last time. You know my heart; you know my path is rugged and this burden is too much to bear. You have promised us that you wouldn't yoke us with anything too great to handle, but I swear to you, oh God, this is too much for me. The temptation is too great, the pull too strong; please take it away. Strip me of this suffering.

I can't live with this guilt any longer. This life of secrets and shame. Terror is my only companion and silence my only comfort. No longer can I handle the impending judgment nor the ignorance of those around me. That which is hidden will soon come to light – I fear both it's occultation and its discovery; the unknown is rotting me from the inside out. I lean on you to ease me of this suffering. End the black night my life has become. Satan is tempting me with his sweet voice towards promises that lead only to ruin, and I know I have become *too weak to resist that which I have allowed to grow inside of me. It has taken root, and it will never be torn out.*

The best I can hope to accomplish is to fight against it, eternally, ever aware that it is inside of me. But this resolve is fleeting, I know I cannot do this alone, and I fear that I cannot handle it at all. Strength is no longer enough – I need you to take this out of me. Uproot the evil that crawls in my soul and dislodge the sin from my brain. This is the only hope I have left. I walk as the dead, in a world divorced from you, and even a glimpse at your grace is no longer enough; I am far too filthy, my eyes are caked with the muck of sin. I need to be washed clean.

✝

With his parents gone, Joe knew that this was his chance to indulge. Bible study was usually a couple of hours, easily more if his mom was in a talkative mood. "So much of the good word and the miraculousness of the Lord to discuss," she often said, painfully. He thanked the Universe for Assistant Minister Jerald's 3rd DUI and a last-minute change of venue. Typically it would be hosted at their house, so there was no excuse to be absent, but with Jerald's house on the other side of town, Joe was able to convince them that it would interfere with his exaggerated piles of homework.

"You'll want to stay and chat, and I don't want to rush your bible discussion. Plus I've got a lot of math homework for tomorrow," he implored. She resisted, but dad agreed, ever concerned with the boy's grades. Away they went.

With an excessively rare afternoon alone, there was only one thing that Joe wanted: Cartoons. Sure, not many of the kids his age were still into them. Most had already secured their positions in sports and/or early adolescent trouble making, but then again, they had all already gotten to enjoy cartoons. Television was almost entirely off-limits to Joe since his brother left five years ago. His parents had thought it a source of corruption and Satanic influence, why else would their eldest child, Stan, so bright and full of potential, become seduced into drugs and perversion? The only reason they even had a television was for religious programming, nightly news, and post-church Sunday Football – of which Joe's father was obsessed. On those rare occasions of use, the mute button was hastily pressed during every commercial break to help dampen the secular influence upon their household.

Joe felt, given his drought of television for the past five years, that even at 12, some cartoons were owed to him. He'd worry about social status, and girls, and not being a social outcast, and fitting in, and becoming interesting in a few years; for now though, it was pariah-dom, and lies, and hidden comic books – taped in a bag inside the bottom of his box spring – and sneaking cartoons, whenever available. If given the chance, there was also the occasional peek at a girlie magazine, a few drags from a discarded, half-smoked cigarette, or the increasingly rare stolen candy bar, but as 12-year-old boys go, Joe's vices could scarcely be considered abominations, he reasoned; despite the deep shame he held for these transgressions.

He switched on the old, wood-paneled box on just in

time to catch the tail end of a commercial for *Jungle Hunter* toys. *Jungle Hunter* was an ultra-violent film about an invisible alien killing mercenaries in the Peruvian jungle that had just been released into theaters. He only knew of it from hearing other kids talking about it, some had even claimed to have seen it. The idea that kids his age had been able to see it, combined with the fact that actual, legit *Jungle Hunter* toys were also currently being played with by his peers sent shivers down his spine

His awed gaze was broken as the opening credits of *Creepies* came on. Replete with standard horror images, the intro panned across a cartoon graveyard with zombie hands bursting through graves, red-eyed gargoyles perching atop short crypts, an ax-wielding maniac stalking through a cluster of trees, and an animated bat that transforms into a cheaply animated facsimile of Bela Lugosi's Dracula. It ends as a crypt door opens with an ancient grimoire sitting upon a crumbling pedestal inside. The book, covered in a nonsensical mishmash of archaic occult symbols and religious icons snaps open and the luminous title of the show is finally revealed, "Creepies," scrawled in cryptic lettering. The page is turned to reveal the title of the episode, "Sabbath of the Fox Devils."

Joe was consumed with shock and awe.

He had seen fleeting moments of this at his cousin's house, before being ripped away from the blue-glowing television by his mother, in a fit of self-righteous, religious fury. Something about a, "...Satanic playpen designed to indoctrinate the youth..." They left shortly after, and from then on anytime they went to Aunt Sylvia and

Uncle Merle's house, time with his cousin, Hank, was to be spent either outside or not at all. No tv, no going into his bedroom, "Who knows what kind of nastiness Sylvia lets him have," and absolutely no spending time with his Hank's friends, because, "The Lord only knows what kind of unholiness they'd get up to."

A couple of years ago, kids talked about the show at school, too. Denny, always wearing some manner of horror shirt, with a rolled-up copy of Fangoria ever in his back pocket, was the first to tell him about it. Denny was one of the only kids who didn't make fun of Joe, and while they weren't exactly friends, they were friendly. And Denny seemed to like that Joe was transfixed when hearing descriptions of all the movies and tv shows that Joe's parents wouldn't let him watch and all the comics he couldn't buy.

Denny explained the premise of *Creepies* to him, "It's sort of like *Scooby-Doo*, but really horror. It's like five teenage punks who travel around in a busted up old Buick accidentally conjuring demons, opening portals to other dimensions, awakening vengeful spirits, and pissing off monsters. Then, they have to figure out how to make things go back to normal and take care of the creatures running amok. Plus, their car has a hidden compartment inside it with cool weapons, ancient talismans, and occult manuscripts. It's totally bad-ass!" It sounded like everything Joe ever wanted and could never have. But not that day, and he hadn't even planned it. A look of glee opened across his face. His parents might be gone for a couple of hours, maybe more. He'd get to watch an entire episode of *Creepies*, uninterrupted.

✝

"Spider, lemme see the book," Skip, short and muscular with a head shaved bald, badly drawn aquatic tattoos covering his sleeveless arms, shouts over the blasting new-wave soundtrack. The inside of the car is animated in the Hanna Barbara method, only filthy and created with a lot less money. The five punks are comically crammed into the car, despite its boat-like size. Spider is in the front, navigating from the passenger seat. He's the family-friendliest cartoon rendition of a junky ever put to cel. Rumor is he's based off William S. Burroughs if he had been 20 during the first wave of 70s punk. He's gaunt and tall with a creaking voice and a big nose that is absurdly finished with a safety pin running through both nostrils and the septum.

James is driving - almost punk, but wrong. Too bright, the wrong sort of chaos and patterns – clashing plaids on every layer, it's almost psychedelic. Skip is in the back, reading from the ancient tome, adorned in all black. This book is their greatest power; it's also how they get into all the messes and hijinks week after week. To his left are Big Cal and Spud. Big Cal looks like a punk rock Solomon Grundy – a hulking monstrosity of a man via a cartoonist's eye for every variety of bodily exaggeration. Spud is the most normal in appearance, with no wacky hair, clothing, or contorted biology. For most episodes, he just sits there silently and smokes, as is the case now.

Skip, from the back, "It says here that there's gold to be had if we find the leprechaun in the Cheapskate Mountains..."

Big Cal shifts in his seat attempting to make a point, his hulking movement results in the car almost flying off the road.

"Jesus, ya big ape, watch it!" James shouts. Cal looks wounded, but James winks at him via the rearview mirror and Cal visibly relaxes.

"Leprechauns are horrible. We dealt with that one in Ireland and I still have scars from all the biting. Plus, the gold was actually just painted rocks," Cal says, with a crystal, booming voice.

Sounds of agreement fill the car.

"Well then we've got vampires in Tucson, which really is dumb, it's literally always sunny! Looks like another Mummy we could try to bribe for its treasure in Texas, and there's a horde of demons in Northern California; otherwise, I'm out of ideas for this region of the states," Skip, furiously flipping pages as he speaks.

"Vamps are always bad news and Arizona's too hot this time a year, same with Texas and I hate the smell of a mummy in the heat, even a dry one," Spider says, steely eyes looking off into the looping background distance of cacti, mountains, and the same wooden shack repeated over and over and over. "Plus, mummies don't usually have treasure where they're buried. It's always off somewhere else, and there are great promises of getting it after you free them from their curse, but do you ever see it? No."

"Ok," Skip, resolved to find something, "I hear ya, vamps, mummies are both a bad rap. I haven't heard anything bad about the demon horde yet? Northern California, a chance to check out some babes, get out of the brutal southern heat, fight some demons, and maybe see what loot they've got. Ya gotta admit that sounds pretty cherry, eh?"

Grunts of agreement once again fill the car.

"Well, I ain't hearing a no, so demon horde it is!" James shouts as the car drives down an endless highway and out of view.

Cut to commercial.

✝

J oe sat hypnotized by the following three minutes of brain-eating zombies, teeth rotting candy, animated animal mascots, scantily clad monster women, and chronically loud voice-over work. So many cartoons to watch, neon guns to shoot, movies to rent, video-games to play, and unnaturally colored junk food to eat. With every commercial shouting and demanding attention, Joe felt wrapped in the blue, warm glow of the television. He wondered why he was forced to miss this, why he was ordered to feel shame for wanting something as simple as sugar cereal, dayglo candy shaped like bugs, and cartoons with monsters in them. The only cartoons he was allowed to watch were the kind checked out from the church library. Bible stories told in drab colors about people living in the deserts of the Middle East two thousand years ago. Not exactly entertaining, interesting, colorful, or imaginative. Not anything like this.

CHAPTER 2

The Crayola sun breaks under the horizon as an unnaturally orange moon appears. The gang step out of the Buick and stretch. Behind them, twisting labyrinths of Escher-esque roads tangle off into the darkening horizon. Looming ahead of them is the gaping maw of a dimly lit cave. The atmosphere is heightened by choppily animated fog pouring from the cave's opening and the roaring boom of a pipe organ. The gang looks to Cal, ever expecting the human behemoth to take the lead into all dark and treacherous places. He sighs and forges on ahead into the darkness, one exaggeratedly ground-shaking step after another.

The ceiling of the cave hangs overhead, seemingly higher than physically possible, given the size from the outside. The gang wander in a way and then cram themselves into an alcove defined by a forest of massive stalagmites. Giant bats, with glowing orange-brown eyes, release themselves from the ceiling and flutter deeper into the cavernous abyss. Brief glimpses of fear are replaced by faux-courage. At the center of the alcove sits a crumbling stone altar smeared in dried red. Its scent makes its way to the collective nose of the punks and they all wretch as one.

"What is that smell?" Spider coughs out.

"I think it's coming from the book," calls Skip, edging towards the tattered grimoire sitting atop the altar, "That or Cal hasn't brushed his teeth since Wisconsin."

An awkwardly long pause is given for the laughter of children across America. Cal steps forward sheepishly, raising a finger, as though an impassioned plea in the name of his oral health's defense is impending.

Skip glances over and winks, "Just pulling your chain, big fella."

Cal's feeble defense posture relaxes and a smile crosses his gargantuan, cartoon face. It's at this moment, with Cal's smile cresting, that Skip touches his naked, octopus-inked hand to the rot-scented tome. A streak of green light shoots through the aged, hardened blood upon the altar and the once eerily lit cave goes momentarily black. As the lights return, Skip picks up the book, which bears the title *Liber Abominationum*. It creaks open of its own accord, and his face ripples with fear. Of its own accord, the book gently lifts from Skip's shaking hands, floating several inches above his face. A brief flash of open pages is shown.

Rough ink drawings of figures in ritual robes seemingly pray while the book floats ahead. We flash to the shocked faces of the punks and the back to the book again. On the next vignette, the ground opens up, threatening to swallow the still praying figures. Then, with the ground open, like a hungry mouth, those in prayer hover above it as reddish-orange creatures crawl out from the hole. Finally, the ground is closed and the robed figures dance in hedonistic abandon with the fox-like demons.

On the second page of the spread, a large demonic fox face is shown surrounded by archaic lettering that follows the shape of its face. Above the head sits a sideways "8," and a cross with two bars juts up from the point of intersection; the alchemical symbol for sulfur, what is also known as the Leviathan Cross. Within the face of the fox, in shimmering gold ink, text appears in the same ancient script as that which borders the cryptic face. Finally, all four corners of the page show an illustration of the moon and its phases. For the top two, below the moon stands a fox, and for the bottom two moons, the fox is above them. In each instance of the moon cycle, the fox is of a different size. On full it is the largest, on crescent, it is the smallest, the other two appear to be waning half and waxing half for which the fox is the same, a middle size.

A look of dread flashes across Skip's face, as he is lifted to meet the floating book. Bolts of cheaply illustrated green electricity streak across the floor and up the walls as a voice, harsh and crushing comes from Skip's unwilling lips. The indecipherable blend of Latin, English, Aramaic, and Tamil spews forth, and the rest of the gang are forced by invisible hands into kneeling positions. As the ground swells and cracks, everyone scrambles to get up, to get out, but they are frozen in prayer. The Earth shudders below and the Saturday morning cartoon analogue of a thousand piercing cries pour out from the deep unknown of the cave and out into the landscape beyond the black mouth. The voices scream across the sky beyond the mountains. And then it ends.

Unnatural silence fills the air, but the heaving and pulsing of the ground doesn't stop. Skip's lips continue to move, but no sound comes out. As his unwilling body silently reads the final word the dirt breaks open and dozens of vaguely dog-shaped stones rise from the rock and clay. As the earthen tombs spill forth from the angry soil, the smell of damp and rot fill the air as the gang struggle against unwilling prayer service and break free from its shackles. Skip is dropped from several feet in the air, landing with an ugly thud amongst a cluster of stones. The rest of the group find each other in the chaos and try to brace themselves against the shaking earth just as it comes to a place of rest.

In a silver tongue, a unified voice reverberates from the mass of poorly carved statues, "Not trespass but desire. Each road has excommunicated you, now you come to us. A series of broken lives and chances lost, we are willing to pay your final grievances. No transgression too great."

Not a threat, seduction.

The book floats down from above and positions itself in front of Spud. A page is turned and the voices sing once more, "Desire is shared and we are now linked. Read aloud the sacred words; release us of our earthen tombs. Delight and revel in our embrace, as we release you of your master's yoke. This act unites our fate, two paths become one, for freedom from shackles is all there is to truly behold."

The voice echoes through the cave. Spud doesn't

hesitate to read the words in front of him, as best as he can. The mix of languages and dialects has him stumbling and sounding out ancient words. The rest of the gang struggles to get near him, to stop him, but their shouts are drowned out by the chaos and he simply won't listen. None of them know what will happen next, but they are all pretty sure that it isn't going to be good.

As he finishes reading, the book floats back to the altar and gently sets itself upon it. The rocks croak and cracks form up their sides, like birds hatching from cement eggs. The stones crumble away as the cavern is filled with grey dust and cartoon haze.

Cut to commercial.

+

Transfixed by the analog glow, by the power of what he had witnessed, Joe realized that he was tensing up so hard that his back and legs began to ache. The next three minutes of inappropriately violent toys, deceptively unhealthy fast food, and over the top action films coming soon, to a theater near you, went by in a blur. Joe just couldn't focus on the neon colors, wailing electric guitars, or potential gratuitous nudity being marketed towards him. His mind was racing, and he no longer cared about the fringe benefits of watching TV. If his parents were right, if the church was right, and there was a global Satanic conspiracy to indoctrinate children into the occult, to destroy his generation, then was any of this real? Obviously, it was a cartoon, but did books like that exist? Most importantly, did that book exist? He didn't have time to wonder, to truly focus though, as *Creepies* was back on.

+

Black fades back into the dust hazy cave and the gang struggles to see through it. As the grey clears, the foxes stand amongst the ruins of their former prisons, three feet tall, black with red stripes. Some carry wounds. Not scars, but dark and ancient flesh mixed with dirt, bits of soft, pink skin dangling off their faces and limbs. Occasionally, a glimpse of glimmering ivory shone through the muck and gore.

Seemingly there is no leader; they stand as Legion, one solitary body of fangs and fur, caked in dirt but ever red of tooth and claw. Their shared voice growls through the cave, "Our debt you have, but one is all we give." Stunning silence fills the cavern as their collective voice fails to produce an echo. The gang trades looks, and then they set their fiery eyes to Spud. He matches their gaze, and in an act of further defiance, both directed towards them and of character, he speaks loud and molten, "We was told there'd be treasure."

A hum comes from the horde, "What greater treasure than your deepest desires for freedom, for psychic chains to be broken, for the haunts of transgressions old and new to be put to rest?"

As the air clears of the dissonant growl, they vanish, nothing left but footprints, tufts of fur, and splatters of blood where they once stood. Cal runs over to the still prone Skip and tries to shake him awake. Before he opens his eyes, he says, "I told you guys this was a bad idea," and he laughs. Cal gets him to his feet and they hobble over to the rest of the group, still standing in silence staring at Spud. Unsure of what is going to happen next, they slowly back out of the cave.

CHAPTER 3

Headlights beamed across the living room. Holy shit, they were home. Joe's body got tighter but he resisted the coming anxiety, he could do this. He switched the TV off, but made sure to then turn the knob to another station, he walked backward from where he had been sitting, using his foot to brush back and forth across the carpet very carefully, so hide any traces of his body having been there. He wondered how he could have been so stupid, but he didn't freak out. He kept the living room light on but ran into his room and turned his desk lamp on as well, opened his math book and a notebook to a page that already had some equations on it. He could hear the slamming of doors, this was gonna be close.

As silently as he could, he ran down the hall and back through the house into the kitchen and opened the fridge. And just as he pulled out the makings of a sandwich the front door opened, his mother's grating voice filling the suffocating air. Joe's stomach churned and he was pretty sure he was shaking, but nothing was out of place, there was no reason for them to think that anything had happened while they were gone. He tried his best to breathe normally and act like he was just grabbing some food while doing homework.

"Tom, I'm not saying I completely disagree, I just don't trust that man anymore, and that's a sad thing to say about someone in the church. It's like the devil has his grasp around everyone these days, and I just don't even know who we can believe. We need to pray for direction."

"I understand what you mean, I just think that forgiveness is the key, it's how we should be living our lives. God would want us to forgive him; Jesus would too - oh, hi Joe, making yourself some food? You know your mom is going to make some sloppy-joes, you shouldn't spoil your dinner."

He stood silent for a second, not sure what to say, he could feel his cheeks and ears grow red hot. He breathed and stuttered out, "I thought you weren't gonna be home for a couple of hours? I was just grabbing something to tide me over, I promise"

His mom spoke, "Well, bible study was canceled, so I'll start cooking now, you go back and work on your homework, it won't be long before I'm done. And that's the last time we're going to Minister Jerald's house for bible-study. I'm putting my foot down, people can make their way here, from now on."

Joe thanked his parents, put the makings of the sandwich he didn't want back into the fridge, and walked back to his room. The entire trip back to his doorway, he anticipated being stopped, being yelled at, called a rotten sinner or the devil's brood. Each step felt like an eternity and he could feel his anxiety boiling in his blood as his head throbbed and his vision blurred.

But there was nothing. No screaming, no crying, no accusations of betrayal or demands for retribution; he was in the clear, at least for now.

Entering the sanctum that was his room, he sat at his desk and stared inward, into the great white nothing inside, the only true source of peace he'd known since his brother left. His lips felt numb and his extremities tingled. It was here that he could think about what he had witnessed. He could explore why it haunted him so. He could revel in his transgression under the watch-less eye of the abyss. Maybe he could free himself from this prison; a prison not of steel and concrete, or even of wood and shag carpet, but of supernatural submission, of intellectual docility. A prison of the mind; of the spirit. He gazed into himself and then there was a knock on his doorframe. It was his father.

"You've got a thousand-yard stare, son. Math problem you can't wrap your head around?" he entered as he spoke, motioning towards the math book. Joe had been too fixated on the events of the day, how long had he been sitting here?

"Oh-uh, no. I was just thinking one out, is dinner ready?" he tried to be as natural as possible, and horribly so; his ears were aflame. His father stopped moving towards him and nodded to let him know dinner was indeed ready.

He entered the living room and sat, trying his best to

eat his sloppy and sides. He wasn't hungry, he wasn't anything, but he knew that he had to appear as normal as possible, for fear of his deepening sin being discovered. He wondered if this is how his Stan felt, hiding his secrets with each passing, dull day. Sitting at this very table, listening to their parents drone on about work or taxes or sports or friends or - more often than the others - God, relishing the secret life that he had slowly been cultivating.

It hadn't been so bad before, either. Before Stan left or was kicked out, Joe was never sure which it had been. In the time before the fallout, life was ok. Granted, Joe was a lot younger, but their parents seemed reasonable and were fun. Church was a thing that they did semi-regularly, but it didn't consume their lives. The family had an identity outside of being, "Warriors for Christ," as Joe's mom loved to embarrass-ingly call them, now. They would go to movies, play games, his dad read him a lot of sci-fi and fantasy stories; they would spend time at the park together. Joe had a meager handful of comic books. Stan would even play superheroes with him. He long forgot about those action figures, just one more martyr in the name of Christ. When they were thrown away, for being an abomination unto God, Joe's mother had referred to them as, "tiny idols," a term that had lodged itself into Joe's young mind.

Joe wasn't sure what his parents were talking about, the dining room was filled with a low, vibrating hum that pushed through his ears and into his bones. He forced food he didn't want into his mouth, passively chewing and swallowing, overwhelmed with the sound and tone pulsing within his body.

Watching a cartoon shouldn't be this revelatory, that he knew. Were they right? Had Satan seduced him? This electricity coursing through him, was this evil? He couldn't rectify that answer or any other. He wondered if his brother had never left, would he be here now, experiencing this? Without a word, he finished his meal, put his plate in the sink, and went straight to bed. If his parents were still talking or said anything to him, Joe didn't notice.

✝

This is the final fight, dear Lord. Your suffering has become my suffering. I feel as if I am on that cross with you. You have not taken my burden, for I carry it alone. I have implored you to remove it from me, cried to the four corners of the Earth for your sweet relief, and yet here I am, crushed under its weight. I can fight no longer, and I keep telling you this. I can resist not. My burden has become me, and I it. We are as one.

You have cast us into the darkest, the deepest pit and you will not hear my prayers. Why have you abandoned me? Why have you left me here, to suffer and struggle alone? My hatred for you is only exceeded by my hatred for myself. As you will do nothing to stop it, the creatures inside will be released, unshackled, and freed. They must feed, as you will not tame them, and I have not the power to stop them. They have only gotten stronger, and I fear that I will never return once they force their way through.

I sit surrounded by relics and icons celebrating your love, yet I feel nothing from you. Your abandonment will not be forgiven. This blood, this pain, all these things to come, are on your hands, not mine. I have not the strength to hang myself, the only other way I see out. If you will not help, then you will be as guilty as I. Where is your grace, your love, your support? It is nowhere and it is nothing. I spit on you. Your inaction makes you dirt, just like the rest of us.

✝

Joe lay in bed, his heart racing. He could hear his parents down the hall getting ready for bed. Occasionally, he heard what he thought was a bit of laughter and a mild shout. It felt alien, there hadn't been much laughter in this house since Stan left. His mind kept turning back over to his brother. He hadn't thought this much about him in one day in years. Why did his brother's absence haunt him so much today? The thought of almost getting caught, of living that fabled and dangerous double-life was certainly part of it, but it wasn't the whole. *Creepies* rushed to the front of his mind. They hadn't caught him. It was a mind virus, a worm that was eating his brain and everything that he thought was possible.

Maybe it was.

He and Stan would watch cartoons together, back when things were better, back when they were a family. They would wake up early on Saturday morning, pour massive bowls of sugar-cereal and watch *Octo-Man* and

Dr. McDove: Space Doctor cartoons. Even with their substantial age gap, Stan still made time to play superheroes, read comics, and watch cartoons with Joe. He still made sure to be a big brother and told him not to let other kids pick on him just because they were a little poor, which he also told him to never be ashamed of. They went sledding sometimes, too. Stan taught him how to skateboard.

Joe wondered if Stan ever thought about those early Saturday mornings, or the sledding, or the skateboarding; he wondered if Stan ever missed Joe as much as Joe missed him. He wasn't mad that Stan left, he wasn't even sure he had left on his own free will; it just made him feel empty inside. And it made life a lot worse in the aftermath.

There was a time when their parents were fun; when laughter and light and hope filled the house. Their world was bright and alive and trusting. Now it was only grey like half the color had been turned off and the other was half faded by time. It was ashen and oppressive.

In the months before Stan left, life had started to get that hint of grey. Something was off, but Joe didn't know what, and it wasn't like Stan was going to tell his 7-year-old brother. Stan and their parents had been fighting a lot, which was a new development; they hadn't really done much fighting until then. Despite Stan being 15, there had been a lot of peace.

Joe thought back on the night Stan left. Joe had been sitting in his room playing monster trucks with his sizable collection of toy cars. He lined them up and drove over them making crushing and explosion noises as he went.

Stan ran past his door, yelling. Joe thought he was messing around and begged for him to come in and destroy cars with him; this was something that they did often enough. Before Joe knew what was happening, their parents both ran by, also shouting. It all happened too fast, Joe didn't know what was going on. Their previous fights might get a little heated, but never anything like this.

He sat there, in stunned silence, not realizing that his brother running by his room in a blur would be the last time he would ever see him. Having not thought about that night in several years, this haunted his sleep and possessed his near-dreams. His head was drowning in loss and hope, terror and intrigue, restlessness and inquiry. The night slowly melted away and the sun broke over the Earth. He had not quite slept but had also not been awake, instead balancing in the spot between dream and consciousness.

He should have been exhausted, but he was elated as the light crept its way across his ceiling and down the wall. He knew what was coming and he had let his terror drift off with the darkness. Knowing now, more than ever, who he was and what he needed to do. He had but one mission today: to get to his local library. If they - his parents, his pastor, his church - were right, his library would, among the pornography, books written by serial killers, and satanic religious texts, have the book he needed to change his life. Everything else was worthless.

In the name of continuing this new double-life he was seeking to live, Joe went through all the motions of a normal day. He got up, showered, ate breakfast with his family, had morning prayer and bible study with his mom, and then was off to school. Through each piece of the morning, he thought of nothing else than to untie himself from the restraints of a life partially lived. The world out there no longer seemed cold and dangerous, he now felt those feelings inside himself, and nothing external would ever compare again.

His walk to school and the subsequent day were a dim shadow in contrast to what was going on inside of his head. He was seeing colors he had forgotten about, feeling sensations unknown prior to this; he felt an eerie combination of restlessness and new possibilities. He was in a daze, but it didn't really matter, people just ignored him as usual. He was still just the weird kid who didn't fit in. None of it even registered. After lunch, he was getting anxious to begin his new life, and accidentally bumped into Paul. He didn't even know he did it, so he just kept walking.

Paul was a year older and big in a way that looked wrong when surrounded by other middle school kids. He had made a name for himself by being particularly nasty to those who didn't fit in, so Joe had had a few run-ins with him in the past. He just tried to keep his head down and apologize whenever he became the desired target. And he had mostly been lucky that when situations weren't working out, typically some interruption would occur, saving him from the inevitable ass-kicking. Not this time, though.

Joe rounded a corner towards the bathroom as Paul's massive hands grabbed at his neck and shoved him through the bathroom doors. Joe let out a yelp as he hit the grimy tile and Paul moved in closer, towering over him like a mountain.

"Finally, all alone with the queer's fucking brother," Paul mocked, making stereotypical homophobic hand-based mannerisms. "I heard he's in Minneapolis, sucking dick for money in bus-stop bathrooms. My cousin said he saw him, down on his knees, all covered in open sores, begging people to let him blow them. Maybe you should go join him and you can do it together. He probably already gave you his AIDS anyhow..."

Joe stood up, staring into Paul's vibrant green eyes. He was shaking; he didn't want to get bogged down in all of this, he didn't want to get trapped in a cycle of punishment and after-school detention. He wanted to continue with his plan.

At this point, he didn't particularly care about being intimidated, or that Paul had thrown him to the ground; he cared that Paul was an obstacle and a large one at that. The years of fear and self-doubt peeled off as he rose to his feet. He told Paul that he had places to be, so if handing out a pounding was what he wanted he should just get this over with. Paul looked into his defiant eyes, puzzled. Typically Joe melted into a pleading, potentially wailing baby at the first sign of intimidation. This, this was something new.

Before Paul could bring down his fist, Joe punched him in the jaw. It wasn't a forceful punch, but it was so unexpected that Paul was shocked by it. As was Joe, who snapped out of his surprise and tried to land a harder blow. Unfortunately, Paul also shook off his shock and saw this one coming. He struck down hard and hit Joe square in the bridge of his nose. Blood sprayed all over Joe's shirt and he let out a shriek. Dribbles of blood ran off Paul's fist, onto the dirty floor.

He struck again, hitting Joe above the eye and one more solidly connecting to his stomach as Joe was falling towards the floor. Joe was reduced to a puddle of blood. His eyes welled with tears as he held his torso and whimpered. Paul swung his leg, to be the final word in this largely one-sided conversation, but he was interrupted when two younger boys walked into the bathroom. The moment they realized what they were seeing both began screaming for help. Then came the other children, and finally the adults.

Disembodied hands carried Joe to the nurse's office. He felt no shame, only white-hot anger. He knew the school's stance on fighting was zero-tolerance when they couldn't pretend it didn't happen. His parents would be called; he'd have detention or be suspended. None of this was going to make his life easier; none of this brought him any closer to the book or his new life.

Nurse Sheryl gave him an ice pack and checked out the damage. As usual, she was short with Joe, having seen him a lot over the last two years, with the Nurse's Office becoming something of a refuge for him from all the mounting pressure he felt from all sides. He hated that she treated him with such indifference, but he kept coming in to escape the rest of the school.

She smelled like 300 cigarettes and that subtle shit smell that trails behind heavy smokers. Joe wished he had a smoke, knowing that Paul was on the other side of the plastic accordion room divider, just wishing for something to stifle the anxiety floating around in his head. He could feel his rage build at what had just happened; at that fucking kid. His breathing was heavy, labored, as he struggled against the weight of his thoughts. It felt like he might crumble to dust under the pressure of it. He wanted nothing more than to disappear forever; the same thing he wanted when he got up this morning.

Principal Horne wandered in, then Paul's parents, then Joe's. They all shared looks: disappointment, anger, resentment, exhaustion, defiance, and finally defeat. Shockingly, there was no look of shame from Joe. The ice pack was stripped from him, his only worldly comfort, his wounds quickly swabbed with alcohol, and bandages shoved up his nose before they all marched in silence towards Horne's office; a place Joe had never been.

Stan had been in trouble often in those last few months before he was gone: fighting, disrespecting his teacher, disobedience, swearing getting caught smoking, being drunk at school. Joe had been too young to know the details as they happened, other than that Stan had 'been bad,' but as he got older he heard stories and snippets of conversations and put the details together himself. Walking into the minimalist office, he felt an odd connection to his brother. They had both sat here, in this office with Horne and their parents, for fighting. Eerie comfort swallowed him as he tuned out the droning words floating through the room.

Principal Horne had a look of equal parts disappointment and sympathy as she spoke. Joe had built up a small rapport with her over the years, despite his mother's insistence that Horne was, "a darksider who wants Satanic meditation and sexual education forced upon unwilling Christian children!"

"Detention for all of next week," was all that registered, he wondered if it was the first time they had said it; his brain was swimming in maple syrup. "There'd be some leniency," as it was his first time getting in trouble of this caliber. He could handle it, he didn't even know if there would be another week, if he would be here, or if there would even be anything come Monday. He put on his best hollow impression of guilt and waited out the rest of the discussion. It was full of apologies and thanks, it all made him feel sick.

After the conversations and handshaking were over, his parents hurried him off to the car. He had hoped to make it over to the library today, but this incident ruined that idea and now he'd have to wait until Monday. With his adrenaline subsiding, Joe became acutely aware of the throbbing throughout his face. They were going to be watching him like hawks this weekend. On the drive home, his father sat in silence while his mother laid into him. Something about, "...the spirit of rebellion!" and, "...this is exactly how it started with your brother, and you know where that brought him." Joe almost started to feel bad, but the evocation of his brother's name sparked a glowing ember in his guts.

They don't talk about Stan, almost at all, for five goddamn years, they never even tell me what exactly happened, and then they fucking expect me to sit here while they drag him through the mud. Fuck that. Fuck you he thought.

All the words he could never say drifted through his

brain. Maybe one day they could tell them to go fuck themselves, but today wasn't the day. But maybe when he had the book. He felt defeated and livid beyond comprehension.

He retreated inwards, towards the white nothing inside, trying to find center, peace. But there was no silence or peace to be found, but something new instead. At the edge of the bright white nothing was a black unknown above. An endless void pressed against his refuge.

Terror scratched at his soul as Joe wondered if this was what Satan was. Not a man in a red body-suit with horns, a mustache, and a pitchfork, but unrelenting, unending darkness. He braced himself, breathing through his fear, trying to find the comfort of the white nothing inside. But the more he stared into the black unknown above him, the more a feeling of peace crept in. In the back of his parent's car, the white nothing settled into a brief, uneasy truce with the black unknown above before the darkness vanished, leaving him in the embrace of the bright white nothing.

A kiss of liberation coursed through Joe as he tried to keep himself as level as he could.

This was going to be one long goddamn weekend.

CHAPTER 4

As punishment for his, "rebellious spirit," as Joe's mom called it, he was forced to spend his Saturday cleaning the basement. What exactly "cleaning" meant was an obscure concept since the basement was fairly well organized, as basements go, and they didn't seem to want him to sort through and get rid of anything. Joe woke up early and headed down before his parents were even awake, as he didn't want to endure hearing all the additional punishments that they had surely thought up throughout the night right away in the morning.

His newly found, meager sense of inner peace and liberation felt crushed under the weight previous evening. Once home from school, he was subject to Bible-study, prayer, and "Family Time," which included more Bible-study, prayer, and being lectured about the dangers of this "sinful road" he had decided to take. There were a lot of threats and yelling, crying and impassioned pleas to God to direct Joe back to the righteous path. After all that, the idea of cleaning the basement sounded like a goddamn vacation.

The basement steps creaked as he walked down them into the dimly lit room. Joe could vaguely make out the glowing light of the morning sun peeking through the garden-level window at the bottom of the steps. Walking around and pulling several of the light pull-strings, he wondered what exactly he would do over the next several hours. Reluctantly, and without a real decision made, Joe grabbed a broom from a hook on the wall and began mindlessly sweeping.

Laid out like an archive of forgotten relics, the basement had three distinct rooms. At the bottom of the stairs was a smallish room spanning the width of the house. It was home to their washer, dryer, and a small table for folding laundry. This area was also where they stored their bikes when not in use. Stan's was still against the wall, a film of dust coating its shimmering green metal, cobwebs weaving through its spokes. The room also held two doors, each going to the two equal-sized rooms used for storage. They ran parallel the length of the house and were half the width, cut in half by a crumbling concrete wall.

It was these rooms that held the family archive. Flat boxes full of report cards, schoolwork, and art from both Joe and Stan were somewhere within. He guessed that some of the boxes also contained mementos from his parent's lives before they were a family and the remnants of long-abandoned hobbies, along with heavily religious holiday decorations, which his mother meticulously displayed with each passing season.

Joe shivered as he entered the room to the left. He had never liked how it felt in the basement; that unnaturally cold, damp feeling on his skin, the ancient foundation that crumbled slightly when touched, the open slats of the ceiling above, coated in cobwebs – both decaying and fresh. Stan once tortured Joe by locking him in the room to the right, the room with the hole in the wall.

It wasn't too long before Stan was gone. The two of them were playing in the basement on a Sunday when their parents had friends over to watch some football. This was one of those occasions where there should have been other kids around, but the flu had kept them all at home; Joe and Stan miraculously avoiding the sudden plague. With the anticipation of other kids coming to their house having built to a fever pitch, only to be smashed by illness, there came a sense of disappointment and pent up energy for Joe. Somehow this got him riled up enough to convince Stan to play in the basement with him.

After about twenty-minutes of hide-and-go-seek, Stan suggested they play another game. It should have been obvious to Joe that his brother was getting bored, but he didn't bat an eye when Stan told him about the magic hole in the back of the basement. Slowly, talking as he led the way, Stan explained that, "This mysterious hole was created a few years after the house had been built when the original owners of the house heard scratching sounds from the other side of the foundation wall. After weeks of incessant, uninterrupted scratching, the old man that lived here was driven mad and grabbed a giant hammer, smashing into the source of the constant noise.

"Instead of hitting dirt, like his wife thought he would, he found a sealed-off room in the foundation. It appeared to be positioned below the porch. The old man broke enough of the wall down to climb inside the darkened cell. His wife waited for him but didn't hear anything after his initial couple of shuffles. After about ten minutes of calling for him, pleading for him to come out of there, she braved the hole herself. At first, she struggled to get herself up into the fracture, seeing nothing but darkness as she made her way in. On the other side, she was standing on the dirt floor of what she assumed would be a small room, only to see a cavern open out before her eyes, with her husband nowhere to be seen."

They reached the legendary hole in the back of the basement as Stan finished telling the story; "They say that she went into the cave, calling out for her husband. A few weeks later, after their grown kids hadn't heard from them, they sent the police to check on them, you know, old people and all.

"One of the cops was fresh out of the academy and it was his first day. They get here and knock, but there was no answer so they are forced to break down the door. The cops take a look around the house and don't see anything suspicious in any of the upstairs rooms; no sign of foul play, no sign of a struggle, and it doesn't appear that anyone has been here in weeks. The fridge is full of rotting food and the cat is howling to be fed, poor thing.

"But then the officers make their way to the basement, and they start to hear the faint scratching sound. They check out the left room and don't see anything out of the ordinary, just old people junk. But then they enter the right room and see the hole in the wall, and all the fresh rubble with the cement dusted hammer. Before they make a move towards it, they hear the scratching again, louder this time, and then the smell hits them. Rookie pukes up his lunch, right?"

"Gross!" Joe said, wide-eyed.

"I know! But shut up and let me finish. So Rookie cleans himself up as best as he can, and, well, since he's the new guy, the old-timers make him check out the hole. He pinches his nose and approaches this very wall. Shaking in his boots, he aims his flashlight in the hole and strains his face towards the depths of the darkness. When his nose is almost in the hole, a hand shoots out from the darkness and grabs him, trying to pull him in!

"The rest of the cops run to his aid, struggling to separate him from the phantom hand trying to pull him towards the darkness. After a brief struggle, the hand lets go and they hear quiet sobbing from the other side of the wall. Turns out, it was the old woman! She found her way back to the room, from the cavern, but didn't have the strength to pull herself through the hole, or at least that's what she told the police in her delirious state.

"After they got her out of there and the paramedics took her to the hospital, a couple of the cops climbed into the room to check out this cave she was babbling about, but they didn't see anything. It was just a small, damp room with a dirt floor. They chalked it up to the babbling of a deranged old woman. The only thing they never figured out was this, though: what happened to her husband?"

Joe was terrified and excited. The prospect of a hidden cave inside their house, he thought about everything that could be in that cave: treasure, dinosaurs, alien technology, cavemen. It all seemed possible. But then he focused on that last part. He wondered if the cave had closed itself off, or there was a hidden button that opened the passage.

"Where did the old man go?" he asked Stan.

"Well, some say he's off in the cave, maybe they figured out a way to close it or maybe he got attacked by a lion and couldn't get back before it closed. But other people think that his wife ate him, and now he haunts this hole, scratching at the walls, waiting for little, curious boys to wake his ghost!"

And with that, Stan grabbed Joe, swiftly and gracefully pushing him through the hole and setting him on the dirt below. Joe yelled, and scratched, and fought but by the time the first, "Please!!!" had escaped his lips Stan was already across the room, closing the door. Joe sat facing the wall, looking up at the hole, afraid to turn around. He couldn't hear beyond the pounding of blood in his ears. He was shivering with fright and cold, but his face was glowing hot with fright and anger. Maintaining focus on the hole, he tried everything he could to get himself up to it. He blocked out all sensation, for fear that he would hear scratching or feel rank breath on the back of his neck.

As he struggled towards the hole, he felt a burning inside that he had never felt before; a white circle of fire surrounded his heart and filled his chest, burning into his mind. This was when he first felt the bright white nothing inside. He could feel his insides become empty, as everything was replaced by a vibrant alabaster that he could see in his mind's eye. He wondered if the ghost of the old man had taken over him if this is what possession had felt like, but he also didn't care. It felt comforting, like meeting himself for the first time. He could feel his mind working, almost separate from his consciousness. Part of him was still terrified, on the verge of pissing himself and struggling against the cold, concrete wall; one hand gripping the sharp opening and the other trying to push through the abyss.

It was like his body was still working, robotically, but the real him, the essence of who he was, was detached and calm. As he settled into this second-person emotional view of his circumstances, he realized that he hadn't stopped crying and screaming. And as soon as he took control of that fear and shut his vocal cords off, a hand reached from the other side and grabbed his free arm. The moment their skin made contact, everything came rushing back and he was no longer detached. Once again, with strength and gentle grace, Stan pulled Joe through the hole. As Joe's feet came through the hole, he swore he felt the movement of sharp hands grabbing at him to pull him back, but they missed.

The moment his feet hit the ground, he was running through the dusty room, back up the stairs, and to the safety of his bedroom. He was so mad, hurt, and embarrassed. Cobwebs and old cinder covered his arms and legs. He didn't talk to his brother the rest of the night, and since that day, the right-hand room in the basement held a special horror for him; but also awe. At his age, he was sure there wasn't anything in the room beyond the hole, but he also knew that he found something new inside it, something he still carried with him. Even with that, though, it still always freaked him out to be down there.

Joe finished sweeping and briefly dusting the room to the left. His mind was elsewhere and he couldn't focus on anything, much less trying to clean a room that was both organized enough and still dirty to the point where there was no point in doing anything, because it would always look dust-coated no matter what. He could sweep the same spot fifteen times and still get dirt because all he was doing was loosening more of the cement from the ancient foundation.

Upon filling a bucket with cement dust, ceiling dust, and cobwebs, Joe made the executive decision that he was done in this room and headed to the right-hand room, the room with the hole. It always felt a little colder in there, which was part of what made it so eerie, but he was sure it was just coming from the dirt floor in the room beyond the hole. Again, this storage area was neatly organized, but caked with layers of dust from the foundation and the open ceiling slats. Every time someone moved upstairs, it caused more dust to rain down on these boxes of old tax records, unfinished model cars, and children's clothing that Stand and Joe had long grown out of.

He did the same mindless job of sweeping areas until he was satisfied that there would always be dust and then he used a cloth to removed cobwebs from between the slats in the ceiling. He was careful to not disrupt any that looked live, opting to take down those that had begun to fall apart and decay. As he worked his way into the room, he felt himself gazing towards the hole in the wall more often than he would like, ever suspecting an unnatural arm would reach out and beacon him inwards, or that a shimmering set of eyes would be watching from the darkness; but none ever came.

It felt silly to be afraid of the hole, to be afraid of the idea of the ghost of an old man living inside a tiny, dirt-floored room in his basement, to be afraid of the possibilities that that implied, and yet he found himself trying to stifle that fear. The more he focused on it, the more absurd it became. Come Monday, if all went as planned; he would be using an ancient book to summon demons to save him from this terrible, oppressive life.

He could beat this, he had to; it became a source of pride. If he was going to move ahead with his plans, he had to face his fear of this ghost.

If his parents, his pastors, and the Church were right, then all this spiritual shit existed, and if that was true, why not the ghost of an old man who was either eaten by his wife or doomed to scavenge a lost cave below their house? Joe had never thought to adequately test the things his parents and church said about the world. How can you verify the existence of a global Satanic conspiracy? A ghost felt a lot easier to face.

He laid the ground-rules: no crying, no running, no pissing himself, and absolutely no praying. He would crawl in through the hole, demand to see the spirit, and then...face it? If he reflected honestly, he wasn't exactly sure what he would do once he saw it, but he'd at least stare at it, unafraid. Maybe he would tell it to fuck off, or he would just quietly turn around, ignoring it, and leave no matter what crazy ghost shit it decided to do. It was a rough plan, but Joe felt it was good to keep his options open.

As he approached the wall with the hole, Joe could feel his heart beating in his throat and his knees start to go a little weak. He stifled a whimper and forced himself to walk at a brisk pace. Above all things, he assumed that if there were a ghost, it would feed off of his fear so it was best to maintain a confident demeanor. With that in mind, he pulled himself up and into the hole with no hesitation. On his way towards the dirt floor, his foot hit something and Joe's veins turned to ice for a moment, but he forced himself to not reveal anything.

At the bottom, he realized that he had stepped on a solitary box sitting against the wall below the hole. He hadn't gone upstairs to get a flashlight or anything so the room was fairly dark, aside from a patch of crooked light that shone on the far wall. After a moment of letting his eyes adjust Joe looked into the darkness, fully expecting to be confronted by a phantasm or ghoul, but there was nothing. Just a tiny room.

This didn't do much to help ease his growing fear that he was making his entire life worse by focusing so heavily on summoning demons in the name of saving himself, so in a way, he felt more fear than relief of there not being a ghost. If he was wrong, if he went through the ritual and nothing happened, he was in for a lifetime of hurt. He'd already made things bad enough for himself, but his plan involved ditching class to get to the library and hiding somewhere with a Satanic text. If it went belly up, he didn't even want to think of the consequences if caught, much less if nothing happened once he did the ritual.

He processed through that anxiety and suddenly this little, dark room that he had been afraid of for so much of his life no longer held any sway. Hell, he reasoned that if it was easier to get in and out of, and it wasn't so cold, he'd consider setting up a nice chair, a lamp, and putting a stash of comics down here; then he'd finally have some peace.

Assessing the room, he let his boyhood fear drift away as he started to crawl back through the hole. But then his foot touched the box again and he suddenly needed to know what was hidden in the damp room. Joe grabbed the box and pushed it through the hole, following after it. As he brought his legs through, some part of him anticipated ghostly hands, but it made him laugh. He wished they would grab at him, but he knew they never would.

The sun was shining in through the windows now and Joe could hear the footsteps of his parents above him. The bitter scent of instant coffee was slowly filling the house. The hadn't been awake long, so he still had a little time before they came to pile more punishment on him, he assumed. He hoped this would give him a little bit of time to look through whatever was in the box. Something about it felt special, deliberate. It wasn't an accident that it was in there.

Joe's first thought was that maybe his dad had a secret stash of girlie magazines, but that didn't match up with the man he knew, plus he thought that it would be an awful lot of work to hide them in the room beyond the hole when there were other places that Joe and his mom didn't really go, like the garage or the shed.

Opening the tattered cardboard box, Joe didn't know what to expect, but his heart hit the floor once the box was fully opened and he realized what he was looking at. As gently as possible, Joe slowly pulled out a bundle of letters from their oversized container. There were probably fifteen-to-twenty envelopes tied together in a stack with an old, yellowing string. The letter on top said Joe's name, followed by the family's address. There was no return address.

He untied the bundle and studied the faces of all of the letters, his fingers tracing his name, and pondering the blank spot where the return address should be. He tried to figure out where they were sent from, given the inking over the stamp, but he didn't know anything about how those kinds of postal codes worked. As Joe went to open the letter from the top of the stack, he heard the upstairs basement door open and footsteps coming down the stairs. He tried his best to not panic, but he needed a moment to think about what to do.

By the time the footsteps had reached the bottom of the stairs, Joe had a rough plan. He tossed the empty box back into the hole and stuck the letters in the waistband of his pants. As he stood up he saw the shadow of his dad coming towards the door and then he noticed that the string was still on the ground. As carefully and quickly as he could, Joe snatched the twine up and shoved it into his back pocket at the same time as he grabbed the broom and got a good distance from the hole. This placed him in one of the alcoves of shelves, which would give him and an extra couple of seconds to get himself sorted while his dad walked across the room. The downside was if caught, he had nowhere to run.

His shirt was back to being straight and he made sure that the letters weren't causing any kind of bizarre bunching and then he started sweeping. His dad rounded the corner and Joe tried his best to look like he was in the middle of cleaning for being punished. He almost fucked up and smiled at his dad, but he realized that would be overcompensating, so he forced himself to be a little surly, but not too much for fear of even more additional punishments beyond what he had been expecting all morning.

With his dad assessing his cleaning skills, Joe couldn't help but feel like his father was trying to search his soul through a divination of his cleanliness. Eventually, his dad told him that he was doing a decent job and that, if he wanted, there would be breakfast in a few minutes, just that he should clean up first. He also told him that, "things are hard at this age," and, "just don't freak your mother out," and, "we've been through a lot," and that he should, "always look towards Christ for direction." All in all, it wasn't too painful, and Joe felt an intense rush of relief as his dad exited the room and went back up the stairs. He let out a hard breath.

Breakfast sounded great.

Knowing that he needed to get the stack of letters to a safe place, Joe headed up the stairs and to his bedroom. He assumed that changing clothes wasn't suspicious as an act after spending the morning amongst the cobwebs and ever-growing piles of concrete dust in the basement. And once he looked down at his clothes, he knew he needed to change anyhow. Climbing into the hole had caked him with all sorts of old dirt, dust, and soot. He thought it was comical that his dad didn't say anything about just how filthy he had become.

He got into his room and gently closed his door. The perfect hiding spot was under the box spring, along with his few tattered comic books that he had been hiding there for years. He pulled the secret pouch out and quickly stashed the letters inside, mixing them inside the pages of his lone copies of *Bog-Mummy*, *The Twilight Fiend*, and *Lycanthropic Darkness* before putting the stash back. Then he changed out of his clothes and washed up in the bathroom before meeting his parents at the table for breakfast.

Surprisingly, both his parents were in fairly high spirits. His mom brought him a plate with egg-bake and some sausage as his dad told her how hard Joe had been working in the basement all morning. They decided that he was still on thin ice, and there would be a lot of bible-study and discussion this evening, but if he wanted to go into his room and be done with the basement, that would be ok. No tv, obviously, and he was on house arrest, but he could go to his room and read, do homework, or play a game until lunch. Joe was shocked at this kindness and wondered, truly wondered, if they were fucking with him. He ate in silence as quickly as he could and excused himself; he needed to read those letters.

Joe got to his room and closed the door. It felt risky to try this during daytime hours, but he needed to fucking know what was in those letters. He needed to know who sent them. And why? Why had they been kept? How long had they been there? Who had put them in that room? He was sure that he wouldn't get answers to all his questions by reading them, but he sure hoped he'd at least get something.

He threw on a Konsecrator cassette, one of the few Christian rock bands that he was allowed to listen to, as they were local and went to their church, so his parents knew them and trusted that they weren't secretly evil and attempting to use the power of rock and roll, disguised as Christians, to lure the youth into Satanism. And turned it up as loud as he thought he could get away with, which was pretty quiet. The first song came on and started with a pretty ripping solo, before descending into a third-rate Winger rip-off. Joe didn't love it, but it was better than the acoustic, singer-songwriter stuff that his parents always listened to.

Anxiously, he waited a while to make sure that the volume of the music wasn't going to get a reaction before retrieving his stash of letters from below his box spring. When neither parent approached to scold him, Joe got the letters and sorted through them without opening any; he wanted a little time to study them. Then he noticed that they had already been opened with a clean cut on the short end. From what he could tell, the handwriting on all of them was the same, so they were from one person. Other than that, he had no idea. Because he had hastily distributed them amongst his hidden comic books, he had no idea what order they had been in originally, or if that mattered at all. So he grabbed one at random.

✝

J oe,

As I said in my last letter, I'm sorry I can't send you my address so you can write me back, but I just don't think it's a great idea, right now. I obviously don't know what Mom and Dad have told you, but I know that they won't talk to me right now, so if you could just let them know that I'm ok, I would really appreciate it. Don't get me wrong, I'm still super pissed at them, but you know... And actually, I'm sure they're reading this, but I guess I don't know for sure. (Hi mom/dad...??)

Things are weird here. I found a place with a few other street kids and we're doing the best we can at sharing what resources we can gather. Fortunately, there's a food shelf not far from here, so I can grab supplies there, so we do well enough. Though the building we're staying in doesn't have electricity, or heat, or a fully working kitchen, so that makes it hard to do much cooking. At least we have fires outside and running water from the buildings nearby.

I wish I could tell you everything, but I already feel isolated enough, and I don't want you to judge me or stop loving me. Like I said in my last letter, don't trust HIM. That's the best advice I can give you, right now.

Maybe it's weird, but I feel like I didn't know myself until I got to the city. Granted, Minneapolis isn't New York, but it's pretty awesome. I'm just afraid of what will happen once winter comes. We'll probably be hunting for furniture to burn to keep warm all winter. But at least I have my friends, and at least I have you. I miss you, buddy.

I also miss mom's mac&cheese. And my bed, if I'm being totally honest. But that's ok.

I wish you could write me back. I'll try to call again, soon, though they keep hanging up on me.

Be well,

Stan

+

J oe held the letter, trembling with equal portions of rage, sadness, joy, and pain. That his parents had kept letters from Stan a secret from him made him want to flay their skin from their bones. This pile of letters, left in the tiny, damp room in the basement, discarded and ignored just as Stan had been made Joe see red. This wasn't an act of protection, it was the first shots of a cold war that Joe had only recently begun to realize had been going on for years. And from the condition of the letters, years it had been.

His heart pounded against his ribs as he slid the letter back into its envelope and set it down amongst the others. Everything inside him demanded that he read more, but his body wouldn't move. It wasn't until he saw splashing drops against the old, yellowing paper of the envelopes that he realized he had been crying.

Pain and anger coiled up in Joe's belly. He felt robbed and betrayed by the two people who were supposed to care about him the most. With tears streaming down his cheeks, he began to feel the burning hot of the great black unknown above seeping into his veins. The silent void echoed infinite nothing into his ears like he was submerged into a reverb-chamber. His violently conflicting emotions began to dissipate as the calm of an eternal chasm embraced him in its vacant warmth. He no longer kicked at the walls of his mind, as they no longer existed, and the torrent deep inside crawled to a stop. He fought against the sleep of emotional exhaustion, and slowly returned the tattered envelopes to their homes, nestled within the hidden cache of his comic books.

Joe tried to focus on everything he had just discovered, but his brain was moving too quickly to catch anything. The great black unknown was gone, and he was left wondering what the hell had been happening to him, wondering if everything in his life had been a lie. As he contemplated this, there was a knock at the door; it was his mom, lunch was ready. He had been sitting, unmoving, in his room for hours.

The passing afternoon and evening went by in a weird blur of too slow, yet too fast all at once, like time itself was both dilating, shifting, and stretching in unison. Joe suffered through more bible-study, prayer, and lectures. He tried his best to seem interested, but all he could focus on was the stack of letters, who his brother was talking about, how he would get the book, and what he would do if the ritual failed; thought the last one he quickly forced from his mind, for fear that he wouldn't be able to go through with anything if there was a chance that this could all end in failure.

After many hours with his parents, he was eventually allowed to go to sleep. The promise of a Sunday full of more Jesus made his skin crawl, a sensation that was brand new. He admitted to himself that he liked the sensation; he liked the taste of sin. Anxiously he waited for his parents to go to bed. Desperately, he wanted to read more of the letters, but he couldn't risk getting caught with them. His carelessness before could have ruined his chances of getting answers, of feeling closer to his brother.

Several hours later, his parents were still awake, and Joe was being pulled into the silent waves of sleep. At this point, he reasoned that it would be unlikely that they would look in on him or bother him this late in the evening, so Joe decided to read another letter. As quietly as he could, he slowly removed the stash from below his box spring and pulled one letter at random before slipping the whole bunch back into their hidden spot.

Like all the others, the envelope had a yellowish hue and was rippled from being in the damp basement for years. Joe crawled back into bed and began reading the letter.

✝

J *oe,*
    The fact that you haven't called makes me certain that mom and dad aren't letting you read these letters, otherwise, I'm sure I would have heard from you. With that in mind, this will be my final letter to you. I hope these eventually get to you. I don't know if you've seen some of them or none at all, or you're just too busy, so I'll spare you a recap but I wanted you to know that Seattle is amazing. I miss home, I miss you, I miss the friends that I made in Minneapolis, but I got a gig working here and so far it's great.

    I don't know what life is like for you now, but I hope

things are good and that you're having a blast over the summer. Hopefully lots of trips to the pool and nights running around the neighborhood with other kids. It's strange to realize that it's been years now, and you're probably not so little anymore...

It's hard to know what to say. I feel like I abandoned you but I had to get out of there. I feel guilt, shame. I just hope that you've kept yourself away from Plunkett and his mind-games. Don't trust him, he's not a good man. Shit, someone just knocked at the door, I've gotta run.

Love you, Joe.

-Stan

CHAPTER 5

This sin that we have let infect every single aspect of society will not stop until it has claimed each and every child in this room until it has dismantled and destroyed the lives of their entire generation. Satan wants to get in their heads and brainwash them up so badly that they won't just leave the Church, they'll destroy it. He and his evil followers want to turn them into a generation of queers, a generation of Marxists, a generation of secular humanists and evolutionists so that they'll all grow up to be abortion doctors and yogis and sex freaks and East Coast intellectuals who don't know a damn thing about a hard day's labor or the one true God.

Satan has every trick at his disposal. We can see it in our lives now. Take a look around at the movies that come out each week – full of violence and pornography. Or the music played on the radio – it calls for idolatry, Satanism, hedonism, every type of sexual perversions, and suicide. "Maybe the toy store is safe?" you may think. Wrong! Aisle *after aisle full of toys based on those very same violent, pornographic films. Toys from cartoons about demons and the occult, cartoons about drug addicts, sorcerers, ghouls, and little blue communists. "At least we have board games," you may be saying to yourself. Nope. Shelf after shelf of games where young children are taught to summon demons, commune with spirits, cast bones, and consult with the dead. That is not the Scrabble that I remember from my youth...*

These toys literally come with a demonic spirit in every single box, as though they are adding them to the packaging while on the assembly lines.

Lucifer will seduce our children with spiritual mechanisms that we don't yet understand and cultural forces that we have no control over; that we cannot fight against. We need God's wisdom and strength. We need to give these kids a solid spiritual foundation to stand upon and an intense Biblical understanding to help support them when they are out in the world fighting the darkness. And they look up to us, as elders and parents and friends. We need to be strong and pure for them, we need to eliminate the things that distract us from God, so they will have role models.

My fear is that Satan's dominion over this earth is too strong, and that if we fail, well, so will they. Lucifer has traps all over; especially in the places we least expect them. Like a hunter, he waits in the shadows, seeking to devour his prey. We are that prey. And while he wants nothing but destruction for us, he wishes to indoctrinate our children, which is a fate far worse than destruction *and death. By His stripes we are healed of our doubt and with His holy wisdom may we know how to lead this generation, how to lead our children towards Christ and His mission. It is through leadership that we will help them, and it is through obedience that they will save this once great and Holy Nation.*

And don't get me started on the elite liberals in Washington. Their boots on the necks of God-fearing Americans at every turn. Their mission is to destroy the social fabric of our society by introducing legislation keeping infanticide legal, taking away our God-given right to bear arms, disrupting the nuclear family by courting the queers, and installing a Satanic dictatorship that will usher in the age of the Anti-Christ.

Though the world is wicked and divorced from the Spirit of God, let us not be dismayed. It's easy to miss the forest for the trees, but there is an end to the suffering and pain; a finality to the disease and filth – our Christ awaits us. And on his Day of Judgment, we will stand proudly before Him and know that our names are written in the Book of Life. With no doubt and no hesitation, we will be able to say, "Yes God, I am here, as your humble and faithful servant, I know I am welcome." And He will embrace us with his perfect, scarred hands, for eternity with Him.

Let us pray.

✝

Sunday morning was worse than ever, and as was his newest custom, Joe found himself completely zoning out and trying to succumb to the bright white nothing inside. The subtle hum that overcame the incessant words carelessly pouring from his parent's lazy lips was the sweetest relief he could attain on the ride to church. Nothing new had happened, but they kept going on and on about how this was Joe's chance to right his wrongs and return to the fold. "It had been a bad week, but he could turn to Christ for healing and strength." For the first time, probably ever, he felt ill at all their discussions.

He had always gone along with it because there didn't seem to be any other option, and for a little while he thought he could fully adjust into the fold, but the nagging itch at the back of his brain always prevented the type of total commitment that things like this demanded of their followers. Sure, Jesus had seemed like an ok guy, and what's not to love about a kingdom of bliss for all eternity, but damn if that Hell stuff didn't spoil the whole dish. Plus, Joe remembered the time before this all; before religion seeped its slime into every single facet of their lives. They were fine before, he reasoned.

Sure, things went bad with Stan leaving, or being forced out, but the time before those last few months was genuinely good. They weren't teetering over the blistering flames of hell for reading sci-fi books or watching Saturday morning cartoons. They didn't dance with the Devil every time they had a day where the topic of Jesus didn't come up, and their irregular church attendance hadn't made them servants of Satan. Normal life was fine; it was this zealotry that had ruined them.

And it was this zealotry that had kept him from being able to read his brother's letters and write him back. That all felt like a dream in the light of the morning. He reread the letter in his mind, focusing on every bit that he could remember. It hurt his heart and he boiled with fury. But he tried to put on the face of the obedient, remorseful son.

Unfortunately, despite Saturday having been half devoted to prayer and Bible study, that hadn't stopped the fact that Sunday was also a day devoted to prayer and Bible study. So Joe sat in the pew with his parents, near the front of course, and tried to sink into the bright white nothing inside. But he couldn't. It wasn't gone, just unattainable. Reverend Plunkett's sermon had pierced its way into his thoughts and seemed to consume his every sense. He was hot like his skin was burning from the inside. The monotonous voice echoed over and over, and Joe felt every single word drilling deeper like unwanted surgery. It felt like Plunkett's sermon was only to him.

It wouldn't shake from his brain; the tone was bouncing off his bones. Joe lifted his head to meet the Reverend's gaze. Plunkett was staring at Joe, directly into his eyes, like he was witnessing his soul squirm. In a volcanic eruption, Joe was overcome with an understanding of a deeply tragic history full of broken lives. Stan warned him against Plunkett. Joe understood now that the faith of his parents was chains, but he didn't think that's what Stan had been referring to. He reasoned that if the last thing Stan told him was to stay away from the reverend, it must have –at least partially – been why he left. Plunkett was to blame.

All this time, week after week of church services and bible studies, of Sunday school and family bible-retreats, the man who tore Joe's family apart was standing up on the pulpit, telling people how to live their lives.

Sitting in that old, uncomfortable pew, Joe's realization made him want to puke and run and fight and cry. He knew it was Plunkett; he didn't know what, exactly, but he could feel it in every single part of his body. This was the man that made Stan leave; this was the man that ruined his life, and their parents had been eating from his hand for years. His skin continued to burn and Plunkett's voice swarmed his brain like buzzing flies. The smell of rot overwhelmed him as he stared into the Reverend's eyes. Joe wanted to burn him to the ground and watch him smolder into nothing. His eyes were made of flame and his stare carried with it a promise of death.

By the end of the sermon, he couldn't focus. He eventually extracted Plunkett's voice from his soul and Joe sat in the silence of his own mind. He felt a block behind his emotions, struggling to catch up. Distance didn't numb them, but it did dull them. He could have cried, he also could have laughed, he probably could have killed; but he just sat. When the sermon finally came to an end, his parents said their goodbyes to the people seated around them and they went home.

His mother tried to talk with him on the drive home, but Joe didn't seem to notice. His mind was somewhere else, some terrible place it had never been. He imagined a thousand possible scenarios for what Stan had been though. Whatever else was going on in the world around him made no difference. He sought only silence. Isolation. The best he would get was his bedroom but with his parents home and a Sunday, that wouldn't be much. His mother kept talking to him, at him, but Joe just sat, consumed by it all. There was no more bright white nothing inside, no black unknown above, only this; only the suffering that would come, eventually, for everyone.

CHAPTER 6

School on Monday morning was meant to be the most grueling ordeal, especially after a grand series of horrible experiences the previous few days, so after his dad dropped him off in the morning and drove out of view, Joe walked away from the school. This was his chance. Joe wasn't sure that his local library had a copy of *Liber Abominationum,* but if they didn't maybe another branch did and they could have it sent over. If his parents, Plunkett, and the church as a whole were to be believed, the library would for sure have a copy; and it'd be shelved alongside all the other occult books, one shelf over from the vast heaps of pornography and books on how to be gay or the bomb making manuals. His brain started to doubt what his heart was telling him.

The walk from the school to the library wasn't long, only five or six blocks. He tried his best to forge a route that didn't put him in front of any of the busier streets in that area and Joe was careful to remember that the police station/firehouse was only a block away from the library. If anything was going to get him busted, it'd be a bored citizen wondering why he wasn't in school; all the more likely walking by a cop standing outside the station on a cigarette break.

He stuck to alleys, cut through hedges and brush when he could, and ran across an empty parking lot. To the best of his knowledge, no one had seen him, at least no one who cared enough to stop him. This was his first time skipping school and he wasn't sure what protocol was. He wondered if anyone would stop him. But it didn't take long before he was at the doors of the library, which was the emptiest he had ever seen it. He hadn't considered how the librarians might react to a student skipping school to come check out an occult grimoire during school hours, but he was already there so he decided to just go for it.

In an effort to minimize risk, he acted like he knew exactly what he was doing and where he was going despite not knowing either. There were whole areas of this library that he hadn't been allowed into, at least since he had been curious about them. And it wasn't a big library.

The whole Horror section was strictly off-limits, as were the Mystery and Sci-Fi sections as they were too close to the Horror. The spinning rack with the video-tapes was also a no-go. Occasionally, his parents would check out a movie or two, but they always chose and never let Joe look at what was there, as apparently there were too many violent and gratuitously pornographic videos. He walked by it and perused the selection. Nothing struck him as particularly lascivious or bloody, and there were no horror titles to speak of other than an old black and white Dracula - not exactly the height of depravity or violence.

Another reason the videotapes were off-limits was their proximity to the magazine selection, which included anti-Christian propaganda like *Popular Science*, *National Geographic*, and the drug-fueled *Rolling Stone*. A few tattered copies of *MAD Magazine* sat on a shelf. Allegedly there was a section of *Playboy*, *Penthouse*, and *Hustler* magazines, but he didn't see any of those. Eyeing the *MAD*, Joe was tempted by yet another thing he had been denied, but he pressed on in favor of not getting too distracted from the goal at hand.

He rounded the corner of the Librarian's Desk and headed into the basement. Of all the locations in the library, this was the most off-limits to him. While, in times past, he had sneaked a peek at the magazine racks and glanced VHS titles, even having gone as far as into the Mystery section to get an all too brief glimpse of the Horror section. But Joe had never in his life even breached the doorway that led to the stairs that headed to the basement.

If everyone was to be believed, the basement contained the vilest Satanic Occult Library that the civilized world had ever seen. Joe had heard people at church talk about it, rumors of cousins and friends and long lost relatives having gone down there; they never came up the same. The information contained in the books found within the subterranean sanctuary of evil was too much for most men to bear. It would break you. This was where Satan spreads his wings and laughs; this was where his followers rejoiced in their own suffering.

Joe stepped through the doorway to meet his fate.

He reached the bottom of the stairs and nothing was different. He expected some monumental change, some Luciferian revelation, but the world was as it had been before he set foot in the damp, mildew smelling room. Rows of shelves filled the small space, it looked to be mostly philosophy and science books - nothing eldritch or esoteric to be found - though he was certainly taught of their evils, too.

Joe walked up and down each aisle, carefully looking at each individual shelf, scanning the spine of every single book, nothing. Lots of outdated science books from the 1960s with illustrations of beakers atop Busen burners and grainy photos of stodgy looking grey-haired men in lab coats. Other entire shelves dedicated solely to books both by and about Plato. Was this a joke?

Just as Joe was starting to feel panic gripping its icy fingers at his throat he saw a small door to he left. It was opposite the rows of shelving he was currently in. He had missed it before, somehow. It had a small set of stairs covered in dark-green tile and an old but solid wood handrail. At the center of the tiny platform was an open door, around 5 feet tall. Without hesitating, he headed up the steps and into the room. But the room was less a room and more a long closet, almost a hallway to a dead-end. It had shelves along the three non-door walls. The shelves in this room had tags on each shelf. "Esoterica," read one.

Another said, "The Occult." Here they were. His panic passed and was replaced with awe.

He scanned each shelf-tag: Metaphysics, Astrology, Tarot, Sufism, New Age, Psychic Abilities, Demonology, and New Religious Movements. There were more, at least a dozen. Each section only housed five or six books at the most. Sufism held the least, with a singular book. Each shelf-tag, each section a new world of possibilities opened to him. So many ideas; so many sweetly forbidden ideas. Titles like *The Epistles of the Wolf*, *Psychic Mind Traps for Beginners*, *Apocrypha of Saul*, *The Sorceries of ZOS*, and *The Void Grimoire*. Joe touched each book, his fingers pleading to let him pull it from the shelf and devour its contents, but his will stood strong.

After having no luck he headed to the other side of the door, there were only two bookshelves on that side, but he wasn't about to give up. There was one bookshelf labeled Magick and the other had sections for Conjuration, Evocation, and Servitude, along with a few others, which he didn't recognize. He scanned the shelves, desperate, internally pleading with the universe and whatever the great black nothing above truly was. "Let it be here, please let it be here, please, please, please, please," ran through his head. On the bottom shelf, in the far left corner of the Magick section, there it sat: *Liber Abominationum*. He let out a shout and from his left eye came a solitary tear of relief.

He settled himself down, at least outwardly, and brought his quivering hand to the book. On picking it up he expected electricity, a revelation, a good old-fashioned smiting, but there was nothing; only his heartbeat pounding in his blood-hot ears. The book was heavy and old. The leather was starting to turn brittle on one of the corners and the pages had long since gone yellow, but beyond that, it was in amazing shape for its age. The cover had some decorative stamping or engraving on it, but it was too worn to see what it had been. Joe's heart fluttered as he turned the book over to check out the back. Just holding it gave him a sense of purpose, maybe of validation. The back cover was the same story as the front, hints of details lead the eye around shapes that once existed but were lost to the ages.

Joe walked through the small doorway and over to a couple of tables that were near the shelves in the bigger basement room. He breathed heavy as he set the book down, being careful to handle it gently.

He sat down and opened the first page. It read,

LIBER ABOMINATIONUM
In libro enim inquinamento.
Semper autem quanto migrare,
Nihil intus in candidos,
In Black nihil supra.

Joe was about to freak out, as he didn't know any Latin until it dawned on him that he was in a library. As quickly and quietly as he could, he shot up from his chair and ran over to the References section and grabbed an English/Latin-Latin/English dictionary. Once he got back to the table, he got to work.

The translating went slow, but luckily he already had

paper and a pencil in his backpack. By the time he was halfway through the second page, he realized that he didn't need to do any of this. Sure, it was good to know what he was doing, but translating from a book with another book when you don't know the language, at all, leaves a lot to be desired. They hadn't translated the book in *Creepies*, they had just read it. In fact, in the excitement of physically holding the book and thinking that he had to translate it, Joe had forgotten to even check if the ritual was even there.

What if it was all made up? And if the pages don't look the same, how was he going to be able to tell if it's in here at all, without translating the whole thing? At this point, he had made too much of a mess of his life to take all the time to translate the whole thing. He started to panic. If the ritual wasn't in here, and it wasn't obvious, he was good and fucked.

How had he been stupid enough to throw away his life because of something he saw in a goddamn cartoon?

Joe flipped through the pages, deliberately scanning each page. Now was not the time to miss something due to nerves. Page after page of blocks of unknowable text; he felt thrown adrift without a lifejacket. About halfway through, the pages started to change. Now, along with the esoteric writing and bizarre symbols, there were also images. They were crudely drawn at first, but as he flipped the pages forward, they got better, as though the artist learned to draw throughout the years of making this book. There was a winged serpent with an inverted star blazing between its eyes, a flock of flaming blackbirds arriving from the burning skies above, a giant white worm with rock-like protrusions jutting from its body sitting atop a large collection of bizarre animal and human skulls. He found man-sized bats and cosmic scorpions; a creature seemingly crafted out of tree branches with a chest cavity that burned in the deep orange glow of embers.

Others were Boschian demons whose anatomy made no physical sense; one was a humanoid with a large beak, two floating rings around its bulbous torso, it wore a brass horn on its head like a hat, and had the legs of a wolf. Another had the bottom halves of two fish for legs which was wearing an overcoat, playing a fiddle, and swallowing a person through its giant nose. Each picture got more vivid and lifelike, as though these creatures were looking at his soul. And then he turned the page and there, staring back at him with blazing carmine fur and depthless black eyes, was a Fox-Devil.

It gazed at him from the page through black slits atop manic yellow eyes. Its ears tattered and beaten, they looked like dried out leather. As on *Creepies*, the Fox-Devil was on the right-hand page, with scribbled text following the outline of the face, although it was missing the weird sideways-8 symbol. Below its mouth, there was an illustration of a procession of bi-pedal Fox-Devils marching towards a massive burning tree. Each Fox had a floating orb of fire alongside it. There was faint Latin text atop the image that Joe could only see if he angled the book a little, allowing the dull fluorescent light to bounce off it.

On the left page, there were esoteric and occult symbols. Joe recognized some of them from a couple of

VHS tape that his parent's owned: *Exposing Satan in Media* and *Monsters, Mayhem, and Murder: How Fantasy and Role-Playing Games are Turning Our Children into Killers*. He had watched both many times, as it was his only gateway to salacious imagery and fed into his fascination with all that was forbidden in his house. There were other symbols that he hadn't seen. One was an inverted triangle with a short, inverted cross coming off the bottom-most point. Joe didn't recognize it, didn't know what it was, but it clawed its way into his mind.

The longer he studied the strange icon, the more he couldn't stop looking at it. He became transfixed by it, running his fingers along each line and down the cross. The more he focused on it, the more he could feel it burning into his mind's eye. It seemed to leap off the page, push through his sight, and place itself inside the bright white nothing inside. His hands began to tingle and his eyes grew dry and tired. He didn't know the last time he had blinked and doing so became a deliberate action that his body resisted. As soon as he managed to separate his gaze from the pull of the symbol, he fell back into his chair and slammed the book closed.

He looked around the room and noted that it was slightly dimmer in here. The ambient light provided by the garden-level windows had been extinguished, as day had been replaced with night. Joe wondered what time it was or how long he had been staring at the symbol, but he could see it clear as day in his mind when he thought of it. Sweating and exhausted, he collected his things and put the book in his backpack. He didn't want to risk anyone trying to stop him from checking it out, so he opted to just take it. He assumed that no one would ever know it went missing, as it looked like there hadn't been anyone down here for quite a long time. Quietly, he headed up the stairs and was out the door before anyone noticed him.

CHAPTER 7

I keep telling you that I can't do it, but you don't seem to hear my cries. Your abandonment will not be forgotten, and my rage will not be subdued. I now know that I can defeat this, but it is through my strength and not yours. You burden us with immeasurable weight and then when we find our own will to fight it, to overcome these insurmountable urges, you swoop in having done nothing and take all the fucking credit.

I will live this life because it is the road before me, it is what I have made it, but I will no longer be your servant. I will no longer carry your poison inside of me. When I was thirsty you gave me nothing to drink, when I was naked you gave me no clothing, when I was starving you turned your back on me, and when I needed shelter you slammed your door in my fucking face. I call you traitor and brand it upon your forehead. You no longer own me, and the sickness you gave me is dying. I will not give in and I will not crawl back.

My life is free, and what comes after that is on you. It's

a funny thing that you get to carry the weight of your own failure for every person who doesn't fall for your manipulative tricks and self-serving ways. It falls on you, that your imperfect creation would turn on you and mock you and remove you from their lives. This is your failure, not theirs. This is your failure, not mine. You no longer own me.

+

Joe ran as fast as he could, but he wasn't sure where he was going. He wasn't sure what time it was, but he knew it was late. Even with supposed detention, he probably should have been home by now. He wasn't afraid of getting into more trouble, not anymore, he was afraid of getting caught. Especially with the book in his backpack, his parents would kill him, or at least send him away. He rounded the corner and almost ran into a group of kids. They all screamed as Joe pushed himself out of the way and tumbled to the ground. One of the kids also got knocked down and the others helped him to his feet. Joe was on his own.

As he pushed himself up and met their gaze, Joe grew anxious with the possibility that he was in for another fight. Having neither the time nor the energy to deal with that, with still mending his wounds from the other day, he motioned to apologize when he recognized a voice from within the cluster of kids.

"Why don't you watch where you're going, ya big jerk!" it proclaimed in a mocking tone. But before he could react, Denny's laughing face appeared from behind the group. Still laughing, he gently punched Joe in the arm and spoke again.

"Hey Joe, these are all my cousins, they're in town for the week. You can meet each of them later. Why don't you hang out with us! They're into horror stuff, too. Well, a couple of 'em, at least."

The group shifted uneasily and a few waved. One little girl shyly said, "Hey."

Denny looked Joe up and down, "Oh yeah! Dude, are you ok? I heard you got into a spat with that asshole, Paul. That's pretty crazy. But seriously, you look spent, let's get slushies!"

Joe didn't have time to stop like this, but he couldn't think straight. The allure of hanging out with Denny and his weird cousins, drinking slushies in the convenience store parking lot with them like a normal kid, swearing and talking about movies he couldn't ever see, reading comic books with sticky, blue-stained hands but never actually buying them: it all sounded like a dream. But he couldn't; at least not now. If everything went according to plan, then maybe one day he could, maybe for one day he could be a regular kid.

"I'm really sorry, Denny, but I have to go," and with that, he ran off.

It wasn't until a block or so that he realized that someone was following him, and it wasn't until another half-block that he realized that they were calling his name. He slowed down and turned, Denny was right behind him.

"Hey, wait up, will ya?" Denny pleaded, mildly panting. "You know it's not cool to just keep running when someone is calling your name for two goddamn blocks. What's the deal man, it seems like something's going on?"

"Denny look, I'm in a rush and I don't really have time to talk about it... Fuck, man, I don't even know where I'm going, but I'm really in a hurry, can I talk to you later?"

"Dude," said Denny, defeated, "I don't know what's going on, but it's not every day you get blown off by the weirdest dork in school. And that's cool, but you say you need a place to go; I think have the place just for you. Follow me."

Before Joe had time to protest and defend himself against being called "the weirdest dork in school," Denny was already running back from the direction they came. Joe thought for a second before realizing that a destination, no matter how unknown, was still a destination, which he currently didn't have. He ran as fast as he could to catch up with Denny, who was already several houses ahead. Once Joe caught up they ran in silence for a bit before Joe asked where they were going.

"I've got a treehouse in the woods behind my house. No one really knows about it because I'm afraid that word would get around and assholes like Paul and his friends would go trash it. Honestly, I haven't spent much time there this past year, but occasionally it's a nice spot to go be alone. I think my dad forgot where it is, it's pretty far back in our property and there's a lot of dense brush and trees around it, so sometimes I go out there just to smoke a cigarette or drink a beer if I managed to steal one without either him or my mom noticing. It's not too far from here," Denny answered, slowly as he focused on running.

"What happened to all your cousins? Do they know about it?" Denny asked.

"I sent them to the convenience store, told'em we'd meet back up later. I'm sure my eldest cousin Mona remembers it, but she hasn't been there for a few years, and I don't think they'll come looking for me there. Do you want to tell me what the fuck is going on?" Denny asked, in a slightly annoyed tone.

"Look," Joe answered, "I appreciate you helping me out, for setting me up with this place, but I prefer to get there first, then I swear I'll tell you everything you want to know."

Denny lived on the outskirts of town, about a ten-minute walk from the library. As they approached, Joe marveled at the size of the woods behind Denny's house; they seemed to stretch on for miles. Though Joe knew that it wasn't true and that somewhere beyond the sea of green was the highway, which they could faintly hear from where they stood.

They headed off into the woods, Denny leading the way. Through they were both winded, they kept going; Joe, overcome with a fear of failure – and what that would mean – and Denny, pushing through the lack of oxygen through pure insatiable curiosity. When Joe could no longer see Denny's house anymore, the boys came across a mass of dense brush and tightly clustered trees. Denny motioned them around the backside of the growth and pointed into the air.

At first, Joe didn't know what he was looking at. He

thought he'd look up and see a wooden box with an open door, maybe a couple of vacant windows, but he only saw trees. He was about to turn to Denny, to demand he bring him to the treehouse and stop playing games; but then he saw the glimmer.

A veiled reflection of moonlight was bouncing off floating glass. The more he studied it, the more of the window was revealed to him, and then the rest of the treehouse. I wasn't in a tree, as he had imagined, but rather was built into and across the whole cluster of trees. It was amazing. Denny crossed through the trees and brush, into the center of the cluster.

"Come on," he said, popping one arm out and beckoning Joe inside the fortress. "The door is a hatch on the bottom of the treehouse, so we have to climb up these trees to get there. Are you afraid of heights? Can you climb trees?"

Joe lied. Twice.

It was slow-moving at first, but then Joe started catching on. Denny was already at the hatch, but he waited, directing Joe on where it was best to put his hands and feet, how to shimmy between two branches, and finally how to swing over to the small door. Joe's legs cramped from all the running and his backpack dug into his shoulders like it was made cement, but he suppressed his fear-induced trembling and made it up just fine, taking special care to heed Denny's advice.

Once they were both inside, breathless, Denny closed the hatch door and demanded, "So! Out with it. Why are we here and what the hell were you running to...or from?"

Joe composed himself as he took in the treehouse interior, his tremble fighting to come back. The walls were covered with pages ripped from *GoreFreaks* and *Infamous Creatures*. Images of film gore, special effects, monster designs, and eerie scenes acted as high art in this nightmare gallery, along with a couple of weather-worn nudie magazine centerfolds. The floor had thick, grey carped that was dirty and mud-stained. Behind the magazine cutouts, the walls also had carpet; an accidentally beautiful mosaic of multi-colored scraps and sales-book samples - a scavenged masterpiece.

There was a lazy boy in the room, which the existence of in a place this high, puzzled Joe. Large swaths of its brown fabric were hanging loose and weathered. It was peppered with cigarette burns and randomly placed holes, but it looked structurally sound, so Joe took a seat. There were a few folding chairs and a card table, which Denny sat down at. The table held a radio with a tape player, a scattered assortment of punk and heavy metal tapes – Joe read through the names on the tapes, having never heard of most of them, though he recognized a few as being particularly evil in the eyes of his parents and the church: Steel Jezebel, Lord Pentagram, and Unholy Saint.

There was also a stack of magazines and comic books, including *Draculina*, *Shredder*, *GoreFreaks*, and *Punk & Roll*; plus an ashtray full of gum and cigarette butts, which coated the room with the grimy scent of stale smoke. Flaps of irregularly cut rugs, which could be lifted for viewing the forest, or put down for privacy and noise control, covered the two windows. For Joe, this treehouse was the most amazing place he had ever been to.

He met Denny's exhausted, puzzled gaze and pulled the book from his backpack. Joe explained about his parents – his life. He told him about watching that episode of *Creepies*, the bright white nothing inside that he had felt for so long and new, electrifying black unknown above; he told him about Stan and Reverend Plunkett, and what he had discovered but what he also didn't know. He told him about the book, the very book he held in his hands, and his quest for freedom, and the symbol burrowing into his brain, and the Fox-Devils. Joe didn't know how Denny was going to take it. He thought he might be laughed out of the room and now that he had said it all aloud he suddenly felt like a fool.

Denny motioned as if to protest, or scoff, or question Joe's sanity. But he stopped himself and asked for the book, despite the stern look of skepticism in his eyes.. Joe opened it to the spread of the Ritual of the Fox-Devils. What Denny saw staring back at him from the page sent shivers down his spine.

He'd faced every manner of demon, monster, killer, alien, and ghost in his days as a horror fan. He'd prided himself that horror had stopped affecting him so much, and now he'd been able to see the artistry behind the spectacle. But this seemed too real. The Fox-Devil staring at him...well, it almost seemed to smile at him. He snapped the book shut and tossed it back to Joe.

CHAPTER 8

J oe didn't know how to perform a ritual of any type. For all his parent's fear of the secularization of public schools being a gateway towards transforming children into patsies of a global occult cabal, he had to up-and-admit that he wished it were true, as they hadn't learned shit about ceremonial magick in his Social Studies or Science classes. The two-page spread had nothing but words and the images of the Fox-Devils. No step-by-step images detailing the process or any handy how-to instructions.

He wondered if he needed to make a circle or a triangle on the floor in salt or ash to stand in? Or draw a pentagram for the Fox-Devils to appear in? It hadn't been that involved in the cartoon, but they were in a creepy cave where the Devils were buried, and also it was a cartoon.

Were the Fox-Devils in a cave in California? Because he probably couldn't get to California and he had already pretty much fucked himself. He weighed the options in front of him while he skimmed through the book for more information, feeling like an idiot for not considering any of this before ruining his life, but didn't see anything useful, just more crazy demons and illegible incantations. Denny and Joe jumped when they heard something heavy slam into the bottom of the treehouse.

"You queers done fist-fucking each other up there?" The loud, shrill voice of Paul came from below them. He sounded winded.

"I saw you idiots running to your little honeymoon shack. Joe, we ain't done talking. I got suspended because of you, and now you're gonna pay for it. So get down here, or we'll burn you out."

The sound of rocks hitting the bottom and sides of the treehouse vibrated through the interior with dull thuds. From below came yelling and war cries from at least five people. Denny rolled up one of the rug curtains to take a peek as a brick came smashing through the glass, narrowly missing his head. He waited a few seconds before peeking again but was only able to decipher the brief movements of shadows across the scattered trees. What he did catch, however, was the smell of gasoline.

Letting the loose carpet fall back over the now open window, he shouted towards Joe, "We've got to get the fuck out of here, man, they're gonna burn it down!"

He hurried towards the hatch, but Joe stopped him, "If we go down there, they'll stomp us into the dirt."

Denny pushed past, opened the hatch, and disappeared into the darkness below as it closed behind him. A few seconds later, Joe could hear him screaming between the echoing sounds of wet impacts, like two water-soaked logs being smacked together. The screams turned to a whimper, and eventually ceased altogether, but the smacking sounds continued long after the last cry was heard.

Not knowing what else to do, and fearing either the same horrible fate as Denny, or being cooked alive inside this tinderbox, Joe started awkwardly reading from the grimoire. Quietly at first, but after the first few sentences, he felt emboldened. The symbol blazed in his vision as each word caused his throat to vibrate with an uncomfortable resonance that became increasingly deeper until the words became one long droning series of tones. And when he was finished, nothing.

Just his heart beating in his throat and the delicate rustle of dry leaves in the wind.

Suddenly there was more yelling from below, but Joe couldn't focus. He felt weak and the area behind his knees tickled and itched from the inside. Dizziness overcame him and he braced himself on the fuzzy wall of the treehouse. Then, he began to vomit.

First came what little digesting food had been in his stomach. He heaved and coughed, unable to breathe or see, as his body tensed with every body-straining retch. Then came the bile - bitter and horrible. He thought that every possible ounce of fluid had passed up his throat and out of his mouth, but it just kept coming. Joe thought he might pass out from a lack of air; his muscles burned under the sustained tension and need for fresh oxygen.

It ended in blood. Not deep red, but pink diluted by bile. Tears dripped off his cheeks as he felt and unnatural pressure rippling through his torso. Something solid began to rise from his stomach and through his chest. It pierced and scraped against his innards, but the object never slowed its trajectory up his windpipe despite dragging against his insides the whole way up. His retching became urgent, violent, and the smell of old decay, of upturned sour earth, intermingled with the bitterness of the bile and the vaguely iron scent of the blood, overwhelming his senses.

Joe grasped at his throat, violently tearing his neck skin, as breath became elusive. The object crested at the back of his throat and Joe plunged his fingers into his strained and inflamed mouth. His gagging grew worse. Two fingers managed to slightly grasp the mysterious object and he wiggled I back and forth, worming it out from his airway. When he had it about halfway up his tongue, he felt a deep pain on the front of the inside of his throat. Something had snagged. He could feel rich crimson flowing down into his vacant stomach, filling one part of his body with warmth from another.

The hot, pulsing pain of his throat dulled mildly, as he focused on extracting its source from his mouth. He pushed it slowly back in and then turned it on two axis, hoping to avoid any more snagging, willing himself to not accidentally slice his tongue down its delicate center. As he unclogged it, he felt his airway clear and new, impatient breath began to fight for existence. Joe stifled several coughs and a fit of gagging as fresh tears dripped off his cheeks. The unknown object was miraculously free from his mouth and he let out a short cry of both glee and pain.

Outside was dead. His ears felt clogged with cotton, hearing only his own heartbeat, inner breath, staggered coughs, and throat clearing sounds. Joe slowly inspected the object of his suffering and was baffled to find that it was, or was what appeared to be at least, half of an animal's bottom mandible. The ivory teeth shone red with Joe's fresh blood upon them; the bone was dull and pitted. It looked old, like something he might find among these very trees, exposed to the eye from the melting snow on a spring day, or caught in the debris beneath an owl's feeding haunt.

While Joe's gaze was fixed upon the jawbone, his mind was trying its best to conjure any reasonable explanation. "Had it been the ritual? Had he cursed himself by dipping his toes into Satan's murky waters? Was this an omen of God's punishment and impending wrath?" among other apocalyptic scenarios, flashed across his mind. Joe's contemplation was shattered as he began registering his surroundings once again, and voices traveled up through the closed trap door.

"Look, kid, just come down and take your goddamn beating. I've got places to be, ya hear?" Paul shouted, annoyed.

Then, "Come on Joe. Get your licks dude, it won't be that bad, we were just trying to scare you," echoed into the treehouse, worming its way into Joe's brain. It was Denny's voice.

"I mean it, man, if I have to come up there, it's gonna be more than just a beating I give ya." Paul again, but Joe just heard Denny's voice circling in his head; the rage began to build.

Minutes ago, He imagined Denny as probably dead, paralyzed at best. The realization of this betrayal made

Joe violently shake; he clenched his fist so hard that the jaw's teeth pierced into the meat of his palm. A previously unknown black hole consumed him from the inside, as blood ran down his forearm and dripped off of his elbow onto the dingy tree house carpet. Then he heard the screams.

✝

I am my own undoing and try as I might, I cannot yet spit you from my mouth. Neither hot nor cold, you are lukewarm and useless to me. I have searched your Word for freedom from subjugation my entire life and found only more chains. At your feet I have placed myself, prone - crying for relief, crying for peace, and crying for comfort. I have washed your head in oil. I have drunk of your blood, eaten of your flesh. But now I find myself at odds with myself, split between two worlds. Am I stronger without you? Can I beat this alone?

For as long as I can recall, you have been my rock, my salvation. You are whom I have clung to when times have been rough and when my journey has made me weary. Through the darkest days and endless nights, you have been there for me. And I thank you for it. But I only thank. In times past, I would have praised you for it. I will not forget it, but I cannot praise. I cannot worship or pray. I bow to no King, not even the one above; and I am in awe of none.

Salvation is within me. I am the key to my own prison, not even you have that key. And yet I don't know if I have the strength for any of this. I was set to cast you aside, locking you out forever. But my heart is strained and my spirit feels sick. I don't know if I can go on with you but I don't know if I can go on without you; I don't know if I can go on at all. At the risk of being the biggest snake in the land, of being beyond saving, all I ask for is a sign. Lighten my burden as I remove it, let us stand together against the sin of the world. I don't even know who I am anymore. I need something from you, but I don't even know what that is. I feel like there is no longer any purpose to anything, least of all my life.

✝

Long after the screams stopped and their echoes ceased their songs among the distant trees, Joe pensively lowered himself out of the treehouse. In the darkness, the trees gently danced in the cool breeze; the calming sway imprinting eerie tranquility on his senses. Once Joe got his footing secure, he paused, straining to hear or see anything. What little light emanated from the trapdoor halted at the inner tree ring, offering him no additional assistance. There was nothing but black silence beyond the wooden fortress. Still clutching the piercing jawbone, Joe worked his way to the soft earth below.

As he breached the ring of trees, Joe paused to allow his vision to adjust. Fearing that he had been tricked into coming outside, he tried to breathe as quietly as possible and have a look around. Soft smacking sounds came from the darkness. They were wet and an occasional scrape followed them. The unknown noises stopped him dead in his tracks. He strained his eyes for any hint of what was producing the soft clomping and slurping. Joe then realized that he was standing among a scattered handful of bodies. Paul's body. Denny's body. Hank and Ryan and that mumbly kid who liked to gross everyone out at recess. Another, whose face was no longer existed.

Shock enveloped Joe and his mind stopped sending and receiving signals. Blood was pooling in his fist as he, once again, hadn't realized that was gripping the jawbone with what strength remained. His eyes glazed over with terror, confusion, and disorientation. He thought that maybe his brain had flipped over in his skull and the world, for an uncountable time this week alone, existed in a context not previously considered. The wet sounds rang out in his ears as the bodies began to pulse and move; but maybe they had always been moving, Joe couldn't tell. The smacking sounds trailed off and the bodies were once again at rest.

Before he could run, or scream, or cry, or faint, or stop his fist from clenching the goddamn jawbone, a mass of shadows rose from within and atop the bodies. Joe felt his muscles tense and release, as a sense of warmth overcame his lower-half. Glowing orbs of orange-red light filled the woods, each flickering with dancing flames, hanging in the air. The illumination of the shadows tore Joe's breath from his lungs and he fell to his knees. Time slowed to a crawl as he attempted to study the vulpine horde that stood around him. Their shimmering eyes squinted as their ears perked up at his sudden fall, and in one ominous voice, they spoke.

"The true heart of desire is heavy and burdened by weariness, we shall mend it for you."

Joe heard the voices not with his ears but with the totality of his being; he heard their voices radiating through his bones. It had worked. Fuck. It had worked. Fuck. He wanted to shout with joy, cry in confusion, and scream in terror, all in that order.

From within the open, unnatural carnage of Paul's chest cavity, one of the creatures crawled. He stood up, on his hind legs and walked over to Joe, licking blood, fat, and innards off his small, sharp claws as he went. From what Joe could distinguish, this one was smaller than the rest. Most appeared to be around 2 feet tall but the creature that approached him looked about a foot and a half. Their collective words were still rolling through his flesh and he could hear their teeth click together arrhythmically. The clicking got louder as the small one stopped in front of Joe and they spoke again.

"This flesh you present to us, your offering, is pleasant and tender. We have not tasted of blood for far too long, much less that of such so young. Some thought we may have been forgotten to the ages. Some thought we would never feed again, but through you we awoke. Now feel yourself awake through us."

Joe could feel the black eyes of the smaller creature burn into him. The great white nothing inside fluctuated and he could feel an addition growing within it. Not ethereal, not physical, something else; like two different radio frequencies coming in at the same time and harmonizing unnaturally. The sensation was overwhelming. Before Joe could react or speak, they were gone. Their chatter remained in his bones, but the only trace left in their wake was the scattered, dead bodies of five of his classmates. This realization made his veins turn to ice, again, but as calmly as he could, Joe got up, collected himself, and ran as fast as he fucking could out of those woods.

CHAPTER 9

Disoriented and exhausted, Joe's burning legs forced him to stop running. He wasn't sure how long he'd been going but when he looked up he found himself in the middle of the small park in the town square next to the high-school. There were outdoor bleacher-style seating surrounding a basketball court and a small playground. This was all adjacent to an old modernist building that was used as a community center that had a large pool in the basement, which the high school used, as they didn't have one of their own.

Joe was still unsure of what time it was, but it seemed fairly late, as he didn't see anyone around the park. He walked towards the bleachers, for lack of anywhere else to go, and sat down. His mind still hadn't caught up to reality, so Joe sat there, trying to breathe and process what had just happened. The ritual worked, the fox-devils were real, they killed some goddamn kids. Fuck, they fucking killed some people. Denny! Denny was dead...

Lost inside himself, Joe didn't notice that Mr. B was standing behind him. Mr. B was the janitor of the school and also did small maintenance work at the community center. Joe hated Mr. B. It all stemmed from an incident where some of the bigger kids were going after Joe and some of the other outcasts. They weren't just punching them; they were holding one kid down and kicking him, hard in the side. Through tears, Joe watched Mr. B come down the hall and see what was happening without stopping anything. He stood and watched for a while, before heading down another hall and out of Joe's view.

After that, Joe started to notice that Mr. B did this often. If a fight broke out, or some kids were getting picked on and Mr. B saw it, he always watched without saying a word. Joe had a special hate for him as he saw him every week in church, playing the role of the pious Christian, only to turn away from the suffering of children. Seeing him always made Joe feel sick.

The overwhelming scent of cigarettes entered Joe's nostrils and broke him from his pained focus. He could hear shifting and heavy breathing behind him and the heat of another body close to his caught him off guard. He turned to look up, locking eyes with Mr. B, who was sucking down the last pull of a filter-less cigarette. Joe's stomach fell to his feet and his breath became short. He wondered how long Mr. B had been standing there, and what the hell he was doing lurking around behind a kid. A shudder writhed through Joe's bones.

Mr. B opened his mouth to speak and before the first word was made whole, a flash of dark fur shot by and tore his jaw off; or tried to, at least. The fox-devil must not have had a great grip because the mandible was torn from the left side, but dangling and still partially connected on the right. It clicked awkwardly in the air as he tried to scream. Streams of blood poured out from the massive wound-mouth combo, coating Joe in hot, sticky gore. Mr. B made a series of short, sharp shrieking sounds, but with every pained breath, the part of his jaw that was connected pushed out a little more as flaps of flesh and bits of fat shook loose, littering the ground.

Joe tried wiping the stinging, thick crimson from his eyes to try to decipher what was happening, but by the time he could see it was almost over. Several fox-devils were tearing Mr. B to ribbons. The blood was so plentiful that it had begun to pour down the bleachers, staining each descending level dark red. For a few minutes, his sickly shrieking sounds continued, but they decreased in volume as time went on, until there was nothing left but the wet smacking sounds of the satisfied mouths of the fox-devils.

Standing up, his own blood rushed to his head and Joe saw stars, but he fought past it. As he gazed upon the tattered body of Mr. B, the fox-devils crawled off of his body and gently cleaned their blood-soaked paws and faces. Once he was satisfied with his level of cleanliness, the smaller fox-devil approached the body and let out a small howl. As if a cue, the rest of them followed suit in a chorus of shrill howls. This was the first time Joe had heard them with his ears, not his body; this was the first time they spoke with their mouths.

After the small one finished, the rest tapered off and the park became silent once again. At first, Joe didn't notice, but the howling seemed to serve a purpose. As their howls diminished, a small red-orange ball of light appeared next to the smaller fox-devil, as though they summoned it with their collective of voices. The spectral ball of fire floated in the air like it was swimming – unnatural and awkward but with an alien grace to it. Beginning dim on the outer-edges, the center slowly glowed brighter and brighter until Joe put a hand up to shield himself from the heat of the flame. It was when he did this that the orb drifted downwards, towards Mr. B's torn body, and turned a shimmering black.

As the burning orb touched Mr. B's corpse, it was immediately engulfed in dull black flames. The skin rolled and crackled as Joe watched the fire wholly consume the dead man's corpse. It seemed to burn with supernatural speed and before he knew it, the flames dissipated and he was left standing before a man-shaped char mark, a pool of sticky blood, and not much else. A few small flakes of ash blew in the breeze, but that was all that was left. The fox-devils were also gone again.

Joe struggled to wrap his head around what had just happened. Before he could, the scent of burning flesh hit his nose and he began to retch. Nothing came but a small trickle of blood, which slowly dripped out of his mouth after his body was finished heaving. His stomach burned, as did the back of his throat. All his muscles felt both tense and fatigued at one time, and Mr. B's blood was beginning to feel tight on Joe's cold skin. He recognized a sharp throb in his palm and eased his grip on the small jawbone.

Putting the bone in his pocket, Joe tried to examine

his hand in the low light. It was hard to make out much but there appeared to be a few holes in his crimson-coated palm. He had a hard time figuring out how much of the blood was his own and how much previously belonged to the now-deceased Mr. B. This brief moment of concentration was broken when it hit him that he was responsible for Mr. B's death. Sure, the fox-devils had done it, but they were here because of him; this body count, now six, was on his blood-soaked hands.

None of this was in the cartoon.

He felt like slapping himself. He had, bafflingly, used a ritual from an old book to summon a horde of fox-devils – fox-devils who appeared out of nowhere, fox-devils who have now killed five children and one adult – fox-devils who seemed attached to him, but he didn't know how to control them, or if they could even be controlled. Joe shook his head as a single tear rolled down his cheek, softening the drying blood that covered his face. He had gone too far.

Admittedly, he had been unsure about exactly what would happen when he read from the book, but he didn't think it would look like this. Somehow, he assumed the fox-devils just had some sort of power, like a genie or something, and they would help him get out of this place; or change it into something better. An unexpected laugh left his throat, as he explored the absurdity of not having finished the episode of 'Creepies' that led him here.

A fucking cartoon.

Pulling out the book from his blood-stained bag, Joe wondered if there wasn't more information within; maybe a way of controlling the fox-devils, or a how-to guide. Thumbing through the pages, leaving red finger-prints on every page, he found the ritual page and looked it over again. He didn't see anything new, but his eyes were once again drawn to the symbol. It etched itself into his eyes and he felt his vision being taken over by a sheet of yellow-grey.

The great white nothing inside was reaching out towards something. Joe could feel himself being pulled up and away, inside himself. Where there had once been nothing, there was now something else. There were voices, the chatter of the horde. He could feel them, he could feel becoming one with them. A chill crept through his skull and the legion spoke to him, from inside his own spirit. They told him that they had now become one. First, the sacrifice had been given, then the communion, and now they were united in spirit, flesh, and flame.

His vision broke from the symbol on the page, but he could feel it burning itself deeper within him, both in his eyes and the deepest recesses of the bright white nothing inside. Joe struggled against the sensation and tried his best to gain his bearings, once more. The distinction of what was real and what could not possibly be ceased to make sense or matter at all. What was important now was figuring out how to make the fox-devils do what he wanted, though at this point he was no longer sure what exactly that was.

And maybe they already were.

When Joe first saw *Creepies* already felt like a life-time ago. He was amazed, watching the mild glow of the sun slowly creep over the horizon line, with what had happened to him in that time. The book existed, the ritual worked – or worked enough – but what was he after? So far all the fox-devils had done was kill, which wasn't really what he had wanted, initially; or, was it? A new life: had that been the goal? What did that even mean?

Pondering these thoughts, Joe noticed the early signs of morning life begin to briefly appear around him. He thought nothing of it, until he looked down at the state he was in. Mr. B's blood had dried hard against Joe's skin, clothing and hair. With a subtle illumination threatening at the horizon line, Joe began to panic. Home wasn't an option, nor was school, so maybe the next best thing was the community center. There were showers down by the pool; he needed to figure out how to get inside and down to the showers without anyone noticing him. And once he was clean enough to walk around in daylight without looking like a murderer or victim, he would need to formulate a plan.

CHAPTER 10

My shame is only eclipsed by my self-loathing. Pride cometh before a fall and it will always be my struggle. The sweet relief of salvation, I don't turn my back on you; I cannot. I have asked for your help to ease this burden; I have struggled and fought and gnashed my teeth and torn my clothes. And I now know that I am my own enemy.

I must lay it all down for you and place my life, my fate, and my spirit at your feet because without you I am nothing. I can feel an evil wind passing through and the only way I can stand against it is by becoming right with you. I blame you not for the weight of my guilt, the length of my suffering, or the scars from my self-inflicted wounds. I am weak, pitiful, spiteful, and guilty, but I offer all of that up to you in order to serve you, in order to fight against the coming evil.

This is the sign I asked of you and I will not let you down. The spiritual atmosphere has shifted and a new darkness threatens to overtake us. As a warrior of Christ, I *will bring the sword of truth into battle and tear down the demonic hordes. Your lamp will light my way. I will bathe in the cool, cleansing waters of your grace and I will have no fear, only faith. My sins are burned away in your holy blood and with you at my side; there is no foe too great, no struggle too big.*

Unto you, I offer myself and let go of the sins of the past. I abandon my immoral ways and shed my weakened flesh. The spirit is reborn in fire and holiness. I will not let you down and I will not fail. I ask only for your grace and strength. I now know that I cannot do this alone. My pride has been cast aside like all other transgressions. For this, I am ready.

Amen.

✝

Sneaking into the community center wasn't as easy as Joe had initially convinced himself. First, the doors were locked, as it was too early for them to be open, and he couldn't just wait out front until the first employee arrived, in his bloody condition and all. After milling about, frustrated and scared of being spotted, he realized that Mr. B had probably been doing some work, before the fox-devils tore his jaw off and cremated him in black ritual flames. Joe wondered if perhaps a side door would be unlocked.

After carefully surveying the landscape of super early morning joggers and commuters, Joe carefully checked the doors on the side of the building. He tried to hug it as best as he could, in hopes of sticking to the shadows and blending in with the brick walls. A few locked doors and he found one that opened, but it just went into a room with a dumpster in it. There was a door in there, too, which must have gone fully into the building, but it was locked.

Joe decided to risk it and check some more doors, but considered this a doable alternative, at least for the time being. Maybe a place he could hide out until the commute and school traffic died down and the streets were a little less busy for a while. Exiting the room, Joe continued, checking the last few doors on the side of the building nearest to the basketball courts. The second to the last one opened to darkness and Joe held his breath to listen for anyone who might be inside. The blood pumping in his head was louder than his footsteps, so it felt silly, but he forced himself to focus on any sounds he might hear. After a few moments, he was satisfied and headed inside.

The already dim room got darker as he gently closed the door behind him. There were warm pipes along the wall that Joe followed with his hand. Within a couple of yards, he bumped into a door. Struggling to find the handle in the darkness, he finally felt the cold metal and breathed a sigh of relief to find that it was unlocked. Once in the next room, he knew where he was. This was the basement level, as the building cut into a hill, and he was in a hallway between the pool and the locker rooms. Chlorine filled his nose.

Silently, he walked down the hall, making sure to keep his ears as open as possible. If he got caught inside the building and its maze of corridors, he'd be pretty well fucked. Rumor was that there was a tunnel that led into the high school from the basement. He didn't know if it was true or not, but he didn't want to get chased into the school or caught in a dead-end.

Joe found the door to the men's room and entered. Being adjacent to the pool, the door led him into the showers first, with the locker-room beyond that. While he was tempted to immediately take a shower, he needed to double-check that he was alone down there, and at least take off his pants and shoes, as they had been spared the worst of the blood fountain. Plus there would be soap in the locker-room.

Entering the locker room, Joe almost felt good about everything. He was about to get this hardened blood off of his skin and out of his hair, and maybe there was a future he could conjure from this mess; a future that made sense to him. But as he turned the corner by the line of toilets his heart dropped out of his chest as he ran directly into the barrel chest of Assistant Minister Jerald.

Before either could react - Jerald to the sight of a blood-coated boy in front of him, Joe to the Assistant Minister wearing nothing but a white towel and staggering to stay upright – the stench of a three-day drinking binge shot its way up Joe's nostrils. Jerald's sweat was alcoholic and made Joe's eyes water. As the swaying got more erratic and violent, Jerald attempted to ask Joe a question, but the words didn't come out in any known language. Joe stifled a laugh, still on edge, before he realized that he had been standing in a dark yellow-brown pool of piss. Jerald had wet himself and had, apparently, been there for a while, given the amount of urine.

Attempting to turn around and go back into the showers, Joe found himself suddenly on the ground, in the yellow pool, with the mostly naked man on top of him. Joe struggled against being pinned down, but the drunk was too strong, too big. Unsure of what to do, Joe forced himself to not scream, hoping that he could worm his way out of this mess, for fear of being caught covered in blood. Still, though, he was increasingly afraid of what the minister might do to him.

Wishing he could control the fox-devils, Joe cried out for the demonic horde to help him. As he was struggling, he noticed Minister Jerald quietly talking. At first, it was as slurred as before, sounding like nothing but gibberish until Jerald's voice got clearer and louder. He was praying.

No, not praying, exorcizing.

With his wrists held to the urine-warmed tile floor, Joe was more powerless than he had ever felt. The booming voice of the minister was drowning out his thoughts as the impromptu exorcism kicked into high gear. Streams of alcoholic spit and mucus splattered down on Joe as Jerald screamed at demons, god, and the devil - often in one breath. It took him a moment to truly comprehend that Jerald wasn't trying to exorcise a demon, or the literal fox-devils, from within Joe, but rather the minister thought Joe was a demon. Given his crimson state, Joe was oddly understanding of this before his fight or flight kicked in and he kneed the minister in the groin as hard as he could.

His knee went right between the slit in the towel that was ever-threatening to come off Jerald and crushed his genitals against his taint with a satisfying smacking sound. Joe was as surprised as Jerald that his defensive blow landed so well, not exactly having done it on purpose, but rather through instinct. He also didn't anticipate that this might make the drunken pastor angrier than hurt, which was exactly what it did.

Jerald's hands quickly gripped Joe's throat and squeezed. Hard. Fighting for air, he scratched at the pastor's hands and cried out in his mind for help. First, he demanded that the fox-devils help him, and then he begged. Asking where they had gone, he could feel himself getting weaker, as his body was slowly deprived of oxygen. There was no answer. His cries got desperate as he screamed into the empty void of his dimming mind. When he had reached the breaking point, as he began to feel a little like he was floating, his brain reverted to a previous state and started to strike a deal with God.

As much as another part of him fought against this, the overwhelming sense in his mind, at that very moment, was: God can still fix this, you just have to ask. And ask he did. And still, nothing, so he began to beg. As little came from this, as had his demands and cries to the horde of demons. And when he felt like his eyes might pop out from his skull, Joe decided it was time to just let go.

Through stifled sobs and brief near-gasps, Joe allowed himself to fall into the silent place within, and the bright white light inside embraced him like soft, cupped hands. The slight tremors his body was producing felt distant, like that of an animal in a cage he was watching. Within himself, Joe looked around at the bright white nothing inside. But it was different than it had ever been. Setting his eyes upwards, or what felt like up in this spaceless, placeless nothing, he saw the great black unknown reaching down. The bright and the dark were meeting, as if their hands were reaching out for each other, despite an infinite chasm between them.

As God met Adam, so Joe met the Abyss.

It was at that exact moment that Joe could feel himself being pulled back out of the bright white nothing, he was being pulled back first into his body, away from this spectral space, and then from his body back into consciousness. And when he awoke, Joe marveled at the beautiful painting that was happening before his eyes, as his focus moved from a shimmering, red fluid sailing through the air, they met the obsidian eyes of a fox-devil who had just forced his face through Jerald's neck, half-decapitating him.

Coughing and fighting for air, Joe saw a room full of foxes as bathed in blood as he. Forcing himself as upright as possible while gasping in blood and bits of flesh along with fresh oxygen, Joe was greeted with half of the minister's body lying atop him, as one of the fox-devils forced the rest of his body through his handmade neck-hole exit. The once white bathroom was virtually coated with sloppy, dripping blood, which the foxes were licking off of various surfaces. The Assistant Reverend's bottom half was nowhere that Joe could see, but the top half was a mangle of broken bones, smashed and scattered organs, and stretched, torn flesh. Joe wasn't sure if he enjoyed what lay before him, and then he began puking up pieces of the man.

A torrent of blood and bile shot out of Joe's mouth,

onto the fox-devil that was standing on his lap. It didn't move. Joe gasped for breath, coughing up phlegm. The fox-devil shook the blood off like a wet dog and then pranced off towards the group of foxes that had assembled at Joe's feet, brushing phlegm and gore from its fur as it walked. If it weren't for all the blood, violence, and death, Joe would have started to think of them as adorable.

He rolled the half-carcass of minister Jerald off of his legs and tried to stand. The combination of the blood-soaked floor and a dizzying sensation that he just couldn't shake held Joe back for a couple of minutes. Once he fully composed himself, he braced against the wall behind as he fully stood. Sloppy bits of the minister, blood, and vomit rolled off Joe's chest, neck, and chin, splattering into the intermingling red and yellow pools below him. The foxes stayed as they were, watching him as legion.

Joe tried to shrug it all off, as it was impossible to feel bad for the minister, but it still made his knees weak and he felt small trembles as he walked back through the doorway leading to the showers. Without removing his clothes, Joe turned on the closest faucet and got beneath the chilling water that spurt out from the shower-head. The cold felt good on his head and face, and better as he drank some, letting it settle at the bottom of his aggravated stomach. Turning the water warmer, Joe worked his hands through his blood-caked hair and tried his best to rub clean his tight, sticky skin on his hands and face.

Having only been at it for a few seconds, Joe felt his heart sink when he heard screaming echoing through the locker room and into the showers. He just wanted to get clean of all the blood, puke, and viscera.

Slowly turning off the faucet, Joe stepped back into the locker-room to see four screaming men staring back at him all holding gym bags. Joe recognized two of the men, one, Ken, was a deacon at the church, and a friend of the family; the other was Reverend Plunkett.

CHAPTER 11

Fixated on the Reverend, Joe felt a collision of the forces inside start to rumble and the chattering of the foxes filled his mind. The men had pained, confused looks on their faces as their screams died off and shock slowly began to scrape up their spines. Ken was the first to notice the torso on the ground, which made his knees buckle, sending him to the floor. But Plunkett was the first to notice that they weren't alone, as the fox-devils came into focus.

Joe could feel the blood matted hairs on the back of his neck trying to stand, as his skin went tight with goose-bumps. One of the men Joe didn't recognize darted back towards the changing-room entrance, but before he could make it to the door a few of the fox-devils were already pulling him down and tearing him apart. His shrieks echoed through the lockers, filling the room with sharp, metallic violence. The moment his severed left hand hit the floor, the rest of the foxes attacked.

Four of them managed to grab Ken and were attempting to remove his skin. Within moments, he already had a few flaps bouncing in the spastic movement as he tried desperately to fight them off. He even managed to pull one off his shoulder and throw it as hard as he could against the nearest wall. It crashed headfirst into it, cracking the tile and leaving a bloody smear as it fell to the floor. Getting up, the injured fox-devil seemed to pay no mind to the blood weeping from its eye or that it had lost several teeth. As it began to charge, it howled; the horde howled back, as if in solidarity.

Before it made it to Ken, Reverend Plunkett swooped down, grabbing the injured devil by the throat. Despite the two foxes at his legs, biting and slashing, the Reverend managed to squeeze hard enough to crush the fox-devil's throat closed. A few frantic kicks were all it managed before it went limp. As this was happening, the other man Joe didn't recognize lay on the cold tile, a pool of blood seeping from his stomach, as two foxes pulled chunks of pink organs from holes they had managed to bore with their claws and snouts. Ken's convulsing body smashed against a bench as he fell into a deep shock, several areas of his arms, neck, and head made skinless with glistening muscle and bone peeking through.

All of the pandemonium came to silence as the injured fox-devil fell dead. Plunkett released his grip and ran towards the door, unaware of what was happening around him. Joe watched the tattered body of the fox hit the floor and he felt the loss inside his soul like he had lost a part of himself. This moment, somehow more than anything else that had happened, didn't quite feel real. It was a dream, a nightmare.

Slowly, the foxes approached their fallen kin. No words were spoken or felt, only a devastating silence. For a moment Joe wasn't sure what was going to happen, but then the foxes started to become slightly more tattered with each blink he took. Peeled back skin receded a little more, wounds showed slightly more bone; tufts of fur seemed to fall from all of them at once. Joe wasn't sure if this was a sacrifice or a result of death. And then, as quickly as it had fallen to the ground, the dead fox-devil stood on its feet - first all four, then just two. It looked weak, damaged.

A low hum emitted from the group; a ritual chant. Joe could feel it in his bones, as he unwillingly joined in the chorus. The fox began with a hum of his own and it appeared to be gaining strength. The single hum cut through the collective hum, creating an unnatural harmony that clawed in Joe's brain. He wasn't sure how long he'd be able to take it but as that thought passed through his mind the chorus stopped. Looking at the foxes, he felt a black flame grow inside his soul; he could feel their anger.

An injury to one is an injury to all.

Joe never knew how much control he had over the horde. So far they had only shown up when they wanted, or seemingly when his life was in danger. Whatever semblance of control he had over them before felt lost in the violence he felt coming off of the black flames they shared. With one of theirs having been brought back from death, Joe was sure that they were in charge now. He didn't know what that looked like or meant, but he just threw that thought onto the ever-growing heap of other questions. At this point, he decided, it was best to ride this out and then maybe they'd help him because it's not like he had much of a choice in the matter.

With this letting go of the reins, Joe could now feel more clearly the link between himself and the demonic horde; he could feel the link between himself and each of them, and their links to each other. They had truly become one. And with this link came a dimming of the black flames. Joe now felt that he no longer had to strive to control them. He also no longer doubted what needed to be done.

+

Dear God above, what fucking evil have I just witnessed? Those horrible things, Christ, they were everywhere. I knew I felt the rumblings of darkness, but I was unprepared and arrogant to believe I could handle this. Give me strength. Give me light. I need everything you have to defeat this evil. I pray for insight and decrement, give me the knowledge and a roadmap to victory, Lord.

The blood, oh fuck all the blood. Jesus! They killed Ken, Norm, and Steve! What the fuck am I going to tell their wives? And why the hell was the Mickle kid there? He was fucking covered in blood, oh God! Was he hurt? Did I abandon him? Oh, Jesus, I need strength right now! I'm confused and terrified, but I wish to be your warrior. I *just feel like I'm falling apart at the seams. Protect me from Satan's advances, Lord! I can feel them now, clawing at my soul, trying to pull me down and torment me.*

I have claimed victory over sin and temptation. I claim victory over fear and death. Through You, I will be vigilant and strong. I will vanquish the forces of darkness that Satan himself has sent. I will cut through the violence and confusion with Truth. Nothing will get in my way. What I did to one demon, today, I will do to all others. Wrap me in your protection, God; I'm going to kick some devil ass. And I'm going to save that boy, in Your name.

✝

With the horde back to full numbers, Joe felt a swell go through the group, as though they had come to a consensus. As it dropped back down to a low, multi-octave hum, the foxes all ran off, abandoning the locker room from every exit; leaving him alone with the mutilated corpses of four dead men. It took him a moment to realize that they hadn't simply vanished, like before; then instinct kicked in.

Joe followed his prey drive out of the locker room, trying his best to not slip on what left of the dead men, and into the stairwell that led up to the rest of the community center. The pack was injured and in a frenzy. This chaos was something he just had to ride out until they calmed down. The itch of fear and anger on the back of Joe's neck became a physical sensation, like a blood-sucking tick.

From the bottom of the stairs, Joe began to hear the

pained screams echoing from every direction inside the building. Racing to the top, he got there just in time to see a woman running by him. Her left arm was scarcely attached at the elbow by a thin strand of stretching tendon. A crimson river trailed the floor behind her, marking her path. Her eyes carried a glassy, vacant look of shock and her jaw was hanging open, expressionless. Two devils trailed closely behind her, scratching away the tender flesh of her mutilated legs.

One of the foxes cut deep and tore into a tendon, rendering that leg useless. When she tried to land her next step, the damaged leg crumpled beneath her weight, sending her crashing into the steel entrance door face first. The impact made a loud thump sound that echoed back down the halls of the community center. The two foxes didn't hesitate in plunging their blood-smeared claws into her back and wrapping their small hands around her spine. Seemingly on the count of three, they pulled in unison until her spine snapped outward, coating them in dense, clear fluid.

Joe headed down the hall towards the loudest of the screams. Between each shout, cry, and whimper, he began to hear the traces of electric guitar, drums, and banshee-like vocals, which got louder as he approached the center's meager workout room. The small mesh-wired safety-glass window and the handle on the door were both smeared with blood.

Pushing through, Joe was met with a Christian hard-rock rendition of 'Our God is an Awesome God,' as he watched two of the devils pulling a pull-down bar from a weight-lifting machine holding several hundred pounds on the lift end. Another fox slid a man's head beneath the stack of weights, right above the center hole, where the pole the weights attach to hides. The man lie still, unconscious, his arms a mashed mess of fragmented bone and crushed meat which appeared to have already been through the pending procedure.

With no pageantry, the foxes released the pull-down bar. First, the pole tried to pierce through his skull, but it couldn't get through all the bone. The foxes lifted, again and again, unceremoniously, let go of the pull-down bar. This time the pole shot through the back of his skull, sending its contents splattering in a radius around the machine as the weights met the mangled mess, crushing the man's head. Over and over and over again as the Dokken-light chorus, *Our God is an awesome God, he reigns, in Heaven above...* sang out over the violence; until there was nothing left of him but dark red slop.

In the corner of the room, a single fox-devil sat atop a woman's lap, slowly consuming the flesh from her fingers. Three were already stripped clean, as it worked the meat off of her left hand's index finger. When Joe was in the hall, she had been one of the voices in the chorus of screams, but she now sat silent, trembling, tears running down her cheeks. A line of drool met the tears at her chin and they dripped onto her shirt together. She sat next to a pile of gooey parts that had once been a person.

Human instinct drove Joe from the room and further down the hall. Blood and bodies filled the rooms as he passed, some dead, some in their final moments. He reached the end of the hall and the main-street exit door. The call of the pack pushed him through the door and out into the morning sun. He no longer concerned himself with being covered in blood, being seen, or with what might happen to him. Now he concerned himself with getting the fuck away from this chaos.

CHAPTER 12

The low chattering of the foxes threatened Joe's sanity as he tried to figure out how to get the fuck out. It had all gone too far, he had gone too far. And everyone was right. He had played in the devil's playpen and had gotten badly burned. Joe knew that there was no way to fix what had happened, but he knew he could run. If he could divorce himself from the fox-devils, he planned to head towards Seattle to find Stan. He didn't know how, but he would find him.

A burning sensation shot up Joe's spine as he contemplated how to separate himself from the satanic horde. The cuts of a thousand claws worked their way up his throat, sending him into a coughing fit that littered the sidewalk with blood; that of both his own and the thick blanket he was shrouded in. Tears streamed down his cheeks as he fought to keep himself, fought against legion.

The hair on the back of his neck rose so sharply that Joe thought it would snap like twigs underfoot. His hands searched and grasped at his pant pockets without his command. They found what they were looking for and slowly pulled out the small, jawbone. The scratching in his throat wormed through his torso and into his guts as Joe focused on finding the bright white light inside. He knew this was going to suck.

With no other idea of how to get them to leave, to reverse the offering and covenant, Joe placed the small jawbone in his mouth and tried to swallow. Despite his best efforts, he couldn't get it to go down on its own, no matter how many desperate gulps he took. As he stood, trying his best to reabsorb the mystery jaw, the fox-devils started coming out from the community center and stood around him.

In one last, desperate plea with his body, Joe took the jawbone and pushed it to the back of his throat, in a manner mirroring how it had first come up. He angled it, and pressed it downward, mostly ignoring the sharp pain of the teeth cutting into his tongue and throat. Once again, he could taste and feel fresh blood as the jagged edges reopened the barely scabbing wounds. Eyes welling with tears, Joe fought against his gag-reflex until it circumvented his control, sending a sprinkle of pink blood and saliva out of his mouth and onto the face of the smallest fox-devil, who was now standing in front of him.

The fox-devil's eyes didn't plead or demand, they merely looked into him, piercing his eyes and peering into the swelling bright white light inside. Just as Joe thought he couldn't force it down, one of the teeth broke its snag on the inside of his throat and he was able to force it through, swallowing harder than he ever had before. Every inch of his throat burned and Joe could feel a small pool of blood collecting in the bottom of his empty stomach. The jawbone kept descending inside his throat, finally finding rest in the nowhere from which it came.

Defiantly, Joe looked through his tears and gasped breaths to the pack of foxes, but they were gone. Small, bloody paw prints littered the sidewalk around him with paths leading to where they had stood, but none to where they left to. The chatter in his bones settled and he could feel himself pulling away from the darkness. He felt the disconnecting of worlds and the hands from inside to the infinite let loose their grasp. And they were gone. Not just physically, but he no longer felt them, no longer felt a drive of prey or animal instinct or pack. He felt hollow, disconnected.

Alone.

With the foxes dealt with, Joe now worried about how to get to Seattle. He was still covered in blood, but with the pack gone, he figured he was at least a little less likely to stand out or be seen. If he stuck to alleys, he might just make it out of this town. There was a truck stop near the western edge of town, and Joe figured he could get there, sneak into the rent-a-showers, maybe steal a sweatshirt, and try to coax a trucker into driving him west. And if that wasn't going to happen, it was at least a place to start trying to hitchhike.

Taking a minute to make himself slightly more presentable, Joe took his sweatshirt off and turned it inside out. It was still bloodstained, but not as heavily as the outside. He worked his hands over his face and hair, doing his best to pull dried crusties of blood off of both. The success was minimal, but he felt it was at least something, though he had no mirror to verify that assumption. Joe crossed the street, leaving the ghostly wreath of bloody paw prints behind him.

After a few short blocks, Joe headed down an alley, hoping to make the most discreet yet direct path to the truck stop. He clung to the edge of each garage that he passed so he could duck around if he saw anyone getting into their cars or driving down the alley. After a block he hadn't seen anyone, having only heard a few garage doors open and cars start behind him as he crossed the street onto the next block.

Halfway up the next block, Joe noticed the sound of a car slowly creeping up behind him. Assuming it was just another driver on their way to work, he stepped into the next driveway keeping his back to them, his heart racing, hoping that they would just pass and not notice the state he was in. When the car reached him, it stopped and clicked into park. Not wanting to turn around, Joe hastily moved towards the gate to the backyard in front of him, hoping to act like someone who lived at that house and that the driver of the car didn't.

His hand was nearly on the latch of the gate when a firm hand grasped his shoulder and spun him around.

"The Lord isn't done with you yet, boy."

It was Plunkett. Joe only got a momentary glimpse at him before his world was shrouded in darkness, as the reverend pulled a cloth bag over his head and grabbed his arms, cuffing him at the wrists. Screaming and pulling, Joe tried to break free from the reverend's grip, but Plunkett was too strong. The reverend's hands grabbed Joe and picked him up. He walked over to the car and tossed Joe into the backseat like a sack of dirty laundry.

As the car started moving, Joe's thoughts were drowned out by gospel music blasting from the car stereo. He wasn't afraid, or at least he didn't think he was afraid. He felt numb, useless. After all this, after the cartoon, the fight, the letters, the ritual, the foxes, all the death and the blood and the gore and the freedom; after all that, he's forced to lay in the back of the reverend's car, at the mercy of the man who, as best as he can tell, ripped his family apart. Joe's rage ripped at his innards. Everything felt illusionary, irreal.

Joe scrambled to make sense of any of it and to come to terms with what would happen to him next. His body tensed as he considered the possibility that he would be held responsible for all the death that surrounded the last day. Sure, he was a kind of guilty, but it wasn't like he'd done it. How many people were alive who had seen the foxes? Plunkett was the only person he could think of. And wouldn't it just be easier to blame Joe and not bring up the demonic foxes evoked from an ancient occult manuscript and everything else that came with that? Fuck, was he about to be booked for murdering a ton of people?

Lurching to a stop, Plunkett cut the engine and got out of the car. The trip hadn't felt long, but Joe wasn't sure as he was too consumed with the idea of his life becoming ammunition for the church.

"A young, once God-fearing boy was seduced into league with Satan after watching an occult cartoon and reading from a demonic book. When they found him, he was delirious, covered in blood, and raving about a legion of fox-demons. He killed 100 people. And let that be a warning to all of you who might think that it's ok to dip into the shallow end of sin, temptation, and worldly things."

The voice spoke so clearly in his head, on a loop.

Plunkett hastily pulled Joe from the car and led him inside a building, cutting his daydream short. Initially, Joe was unsure of where he was until he got a whiff of the place and heard a familiar soft sobbing from another room. Home. Plunkett had brought him home. Another set of hands grabbed him and they led him to the living room, sitting him down on the floor. A set of keys jangled as the bag was removed.

"Is it true?!?! Is it true you're serving Satan? Did you have those men killed; you have to tell me! Why were you with demons?" Joe's mother half-sobbed, half-screamed at him. Joe was sitting in the middle of the living room, but everything had been taken out of it and there were white sheets on all the walls, the floor, the ceiling, and draped over all the doors and windows. On the far end of the room there was a small table, also draped in white. It held a large, ornate crucifix, a bible, a small bottle of oil, and a bottle of water.

As Joe's mother pleaded with him for answers, Plunkett pulled her away, warning her not to talk with, "it." He implored her that she wasn't speaking to her son, but to the demon inside. They needed to get the demon, or demons out, and then they could talk to Joe and get to the bottom of this. Stifling tears, Joe's mom stopped with the questions, leaning on Joe's dad for comfort.

Plunkett joined them in a half-circle and they began to pray.

"Dear merciful God, we ask that you cleanse us right now, of all our sins, our doubts, and our pride. Let your Spirit rain down on us and anoint us with your presence, as I anoint our heads in oil."

Reaching over to the makeshift altar, Plunkett picked up the small bottle of oil and dripped a small amount onto his fingers. As he continued the prayer, he dabbed a small amount of the oil on his forehead, as well as the foreheads of Joe's parents. A subtle scent of olive-oil kissed Joe's nostrils. Wrapping that up, Plunkett returned to Joe and pressed a small mark of oil onto his forehead, the whole time speaking in Pentecostal tongues.

Unsure of what was going to happen, Joe thought about making a break for it. Having an exorcism done to him didn't sound like something he wanted, but mostly he was just exhausted. But his rage wouldn't let him run; it needed to let this happen. Maybe he could finally get some fucking answers, so he just blurted it out, "What did you do to my fucking brother?"

Momentarily, the reverend looked aghast but quickly covered it with his Godly veneer, telling Joe's parents to not listen to a word that the foul creature inside Joe says. He told them that it was trying to drive a wedge between them so it could hold on to Joe. Joe's rage had lessened since the car, but hearing that made anger swell inside him until he thought he would burst. He shot up from the ground and went for the reverend, cursing him with every foul word, every forbidden saying, and every rotten tongue.

Plunkett had the strength of a grown man, though, and pushed him back into the wall, praying loudly as to drown out Joe's blasphemies. For a moment, Joe felt like he was playing the role of a possessed person. He assumed that this is exactly what they would want: physically aggressive and with a mouthful of transgressions. But he wasn't playing a part; he was furious. Somehow, he landed a blow on Plunkett's nose, splashing blood across the white sheet behind him and running down the reverend's face, onto his shirt. This caught them both by surprise.

Without a moment's hesitation, the reverend struck back, knocking Joe to the floor. Joe's parents began to protest, trying to get between Plunkett and their son, but the reverend cut them off, telling them that it wasn't their son he was hitting, but the demon, and that sometimes exorcisms get violent, it's part of the territory. Joe hit the floor but felt nothing but detachment and blistering rage.

He had tried to get away from this, tried to leave this life behind, and he turned his back on the one thing that was helping him divorce himself from all the madness, the guilt, the shame, and the oppression. Joe tried to remember when his life was good, when Stan was around; when they were still a family. He remembered how his parents were, as well-rounded, happy people, not the kind of husks that would watch their youngest son get punched by a grown man and not do anything about it.

Stan. He thought about Stan and how they had driven him away, hidden him from Joe, hidden those letters in the damp hole in the basement, leaving them there to rot. Plunkett reached down to Joe and pressed a golden crucifix onto his forehead, demanding the demons come out. Joe wanted to laugh, but he was too fucking mad. This man ruined everything. He tried to lash out again, but before he could both his parents rushed over and helped the reverend hold him down. Rage turned to sorrow turned to a sense of betrayal.

A familiar tremor went through Joe. He knew he had been scared before, but he needed them now. Without the book, he didn't know if he could evoke the fox-devils, but he had to at least try. While Plunkett and his parents held him down, shouting scripture and prayers in his face, Joe cried out for the foxes to come back to him, which the exorcism crew took as a sign that things were going in the right direction.

Nothing happened as Joe folded in desperation. Despite the distraction of the exorcism, Joe tried reaching back into the bright white light within, hoping he could force it to become one with the great black nothing, as they had been tied together before, but there was nothing. His rage got him part of the way there, but he couldn't grasp onto anything inside. As he was starting to lose hope, he felt a familiar feeling in his chest.

Sharp piercing pain replaced all other sensations as he could feel the small jawbone tear its way up his torso and into his throat. Much to his parent's surprise, he started coughing up pale flecks of blood, which dotted the white sheets of the floor below them all. Plunkett looked at him, baffled, and started praying louder, as though it would counteract the spitting of blood.

Like before, Joe felt the prick of a sharp tooth at the furthest possible point on his tongue. As gently as he could, and despite the manic screaming of the preacher and Joe's parents, who had joined in the mayhem, Joe brought his cuffed hands to his face and grabbed ahold of the small jawbone, slowly removing it from his mouth.

A massive chill went through the room as the foxes entered from behind the white sheets covering the doorways. The room was silent as Joe's parents tried to make sense of what was happening. But Plunkett seemed ready for this possibility. Slowly, he walked over to the table and reached for the crucifix. Initially, Joe thought the reverend was going to pick it up and use it for a weapon, but from behind it, he pulled a snub-nosed revolver and began firing at the foxes.

They scattered as he pulled the trigger over and over, four crumpling to the ground in pools of black blood. Joe's fight or flight instincts flooded his brain and he leaped up towards the reverend, who was trying to reload the gun. A whiff of hot salt and metal scorched Joe's nose as he collided into Plunkett, sending them both to the floor, the gun and several rounds scattering across the floor. For lack of any other weapon, Joe slammed the small jawbone into the preacher's face. It pierced into his cheek and hung there, awkwardly.

Before he could strike again, Joe's father tore him off the whimpering preacher. The moment he touched him, the remaining foxes pounced on his dad and all his years of anger towards him came to a boil as Joe screamed, "You fucking did this! You drove Stan away and ruined our fucking lives!" his shrill voice tearing through his ragged throat, sending specks of blood onto the floor below him.

The scent of iron hit the air as one of the foxes clawed at Joe's dad's throat, as if it was trying to dig into his windpipe. He gasped and wheezed, trying his best to fight them off, but they were on every limb, gnawing at his bones and mutilating his flesh. The one at his throat managed to clear most of the delicate, pink tissue from around his windpipe and started tugging on it. With eyes rolling back, Joe's father began to gargle and shudder as he fell to his knees. The fox attached to his right arm had carved a crater through his forearm and was pressing its nose between his radius and ulna, licking and manically chopping at the bits of tender muscle, snapping tendon, and stingy nerves between them.

A shudder moved through Joe as tears streamed down his cheeks. He hadn't meant to do it. He hadn't meant for any of this. Ice pulsed in his veins as he looked towards his mother, praying that his rage hadn't made the fox-devils eviscerate her, as well.

She was slumped in a corner, blood slowly trickling from a wound in the center of her chest.

Plunkett had shot her.

An all-consuming cold fire churned in Joe's heart.

Turning around to deal with Plunkett, Joe was surprised to see that he was gone, leaving the jawbone in a small pool of blood that trailed out through one of the sheet-draped doorways. He'd have to pay, but Joe realized that they had to deal with the four wounded fox-devils first.

While Joe retrieved the jawbone, the horde had dragged the four limp corpses together and surrounded them, chattering together. A silence fell over the group, as they stood statuesque, as before, and slowly became more tattered. Joe could feel it inside, and out, as scratches and fresh injuries appeared on his arms and legs. From the foxes, more glistening bone could be seen, more scars and gouges appeared. The four once dead foxes stood up and shook themselves off, sending splatters of black blood and four spent bullets across the room.

As Joe approached the bodies of his parents, a solitary tear dripped from his eye. He knew this hadn't needed to happen. He felt so much anger towards them. They could have stayed the family that he remembered, but a poison seeped in and ruined that. Grief clutched at his heart, but anger still burned through his soul.

Joe pulled the keys from his father's pockets and uncuffed himself with an old handcuff key that came with a set of cuffs Joe got for his 8th birthday. Pain moved through him. He had done this. How had he done this?

He grabbed one of the sheets and tore it off the wall, gently covering the bodies of his mother and father. The pack chattered in his mind, uneasy and still frenzied. Joe felt between worlds. Between lives.

Joe's mind disconnected from what had just happened, but his heart filled with equal parts rage, sorrow, guilt, relief, and liberation. He had held onto this anger for so long, he could finally let them go. Tears streamed down his blood-caked cheeks, as he looked at the sheet-covered bodies of his parents. Maybe he had always wanted this, but maybe he didn't want it anymore - though he couldn't deny that some part of him still did.

CHAPTER 13

Oh God, what have I allowed to happen! Fuck. Oh fuck. Oh my god. Fuck.

I left them. Jesus fuck. I left them to die, just like the other men, my friends. Fuck. Holy fuck. They're all dead. What the fuck?

I need protection, Dear God, please forgive me and give me renewed strength to deal with this unholy threat. No longer just spiritual, dear sweet Jesus. Please grant me courage and strength. Give me wisdom and protection, my Lord. What the shit?

Fuck.

Fuck.

Oh God, I am so sorry for my weakness, for my sin. I am so sorry for my fear and doubt and anger at you. Protect us all. Anoint us in fire and your blood and holy wrath.

I have to stop the child.

Oh dear God, what have I done? What the fuck have I fucking done?

A lifetime of sin come back to haunt me. Have I brought this upon us, God? Am I to blame? Has my weakness and sin manifested this evil?

I tried to save him, God. I was weak. I was too weak to save him and I corrupted his mind. I corrupted his fucking mind...My sin infected him and I turned him into an abomination. Oh fuck oh God.

There is a reason behind this evil, that it comes in the form of his brother. Oh dear God, what the fuck have I done?

What the fuck?

+

Sirens cried off in the distance as Joe and the fox-devils headed out the backdoor of his house, a crackle of black flames just beginning to build in the center of the living room. They needed to get to Plunkett, though Joe wasn't sure exactly where the reverend lived, but he knew that he'd have to show up at the church at some point, so they headed in its direction. And if he didn't come, they'd burn the place to the ground to get his attention.

More than any other time before this, Joe felt in tune with the horde. They weren't leading him as much as their instincts had merged into a shared consciousness; it no longer overwhelmed him. As a pack, they walked down the alley and made their way towards the church. As they got closer to the center of town, Joe spotted the high school in the distance. Part of him wanted to go another way, to avoid being seen, but he knew that this was the quickest route.

The hairs on the back of his neck itched at his spine as he felt the chatter of the horde and was engulfed in a black flame of rage. They were within eyesight of the reverend with the steeple of the church now visible as they approached the school. Plunkett had injured them. He had injured Joe. He had been the force that made Stan leave. He had washed their family in madness. A howl shook through the pack; it was the sound of legion. And they had prey to hunt.

Hoping to get past the school as quickly as possible, Joe began jogging, the foxes dropped to all fours to keep pace. Moving as one unit, they ran along the south end of the high school. A group of students looked up from the circle they were standing in, at the edge of the building, and started shouting. Some were running away, others started at the pack, baffled by what they were seeing.

One of the boys, Greg, the brother of one of Joe's classmates, ran up to the horde and started shouting. With a confused look on his face, he awkwardly tried to kick one of the foxes. Before he could make an impact four foxes pounced on him. Screaming into the mostly empty street, the foxes made fast work of him, doing their best to tear his rib cage from his torso. His screams shook in panic as two of the foxes ripped as hard as they could, bringing pieces of ribs with their tumbling bodies as they fell to the blacktop.

Greg hit the ground on his back, hard, with the other two fox-devils taking the place of the two that fell; but instead of working at his rib cage, they tore at his lungs. Their hands pulled dark pink chunks of tissue from the small holes in his torso as he convulsed and coughed up blood. It didn't take long before he was silent, unmoving and the foxes became disinterested. They took a moment to wash their reddened claws before the pack shot towards the horrified students who stood watching, terrified and screaming.

The closest group of kids tried to scatter, but only a few got away and behind the doors of the school before the horde reached them. The foxes descended on the kids with black flames growing in their eyes. Joe felt a hot chill crawl up his spine as he felt the instincts of the pack. After healing four, they were hungry.

And an injury to one was an injury to all.

The group of students who hadn't made it to the school were surrounded by the blood-caked demons. A sense of supernatural calm overtook Joe as the horde attacked the confused teenagers. Arching sprays of blood painted across the sky before splashing on the cement walkway and the brick walls of the school. Ribbons of flesh and chunks of meat flew and tumbled from within the fleshy mound of gore. What had once been 7, or so, students, was now a writhing, shrieking mass of innards and violence. They were no longer students, no longer children, no longer human; they were simply pain.

Joe didn't feel anything but the call of the pack. Where there would once have been shock, fear, and horror, there was now instinct. The cries, shouts, and screeches of agony from the students had caught the ears of other people within the school, many of whom now gathered on the other side of the glass doors; their faces heavy with shock, some having collapsed in tears or terror.

A whistle rang through the still morning air, piercing into the ears of the devils. Joe could feel the hairs on the nape of their necks rise, collectively; as did his own. From around the corner of the other end of the school, he saw a group of teachers and students running towards the commotion. As they got closer, they paused to try to put together what they were seeing: a blood-soaked boy with a pack of bipedal fox-like creatures, and gore everywhere.

The high-school principal was at the head of the group, trying to make sense of the chaos in front of him. Joe recognized him from Stan's descriptions. He was thin and tall, wearing an ill-fitting brown suit, and sporting a greying madman's beard. Before he, or the other folks with him, could react to what they had come across, the horde pounced on them.

Already glistening with the blood of so many others in the morning light, the devils tore through the small crowd. The smallest fox jumped on the principal's chest, sending him careening back into the group where he landed on his ass. Still attached, the small fox went straight for the bearded man's throat. There wasn't much chewing or gnawing, just a few snaps as the principal's beard, face, and torso were painted with rich, thick red. He tried to put up a fight, but his arms went limp as he tried to raise them.

Despite the principal being dead, the small fox continued to snap and cut at the muscles, tendons, and bones of the dead man's neck. After a few seconds, a satisfying crunch-snap combination could be heard as the devil rose to his feet, standing atop his prey's torso, and clutching the principal's severed head in his little, dripping paws. With as close to a smile as the fox-devils could get, he greedily licked at the blood dripping from the open neck.

The rest of the crowd fared no better, with foxes making quick work of once breathing humans, again turning them into a pile of unidentifiable gore. One fox had his paws jammed into both earholes of a young woman, pulling out tender bits of pink from her head and slurping it down like a delicacy. Another fox was simply rolling in the viscera, trying his best to mask his musk with the scent of fresh blood.

Looking upwards, Joe could see horrified faces staring down at them from the windows above. The last thing they needed was for this distraction to lead to even more attention, and with it, more distraction. With the foxes returning to his side, Joe forged on towards the church. This would end today.

CHAPTER 14

After what had just happened, Joe thought they should be more concerned about being seen, but he paid no mind to the few people who drove by, as none of them stopped. He caught the wide eyes of a small child in the back of one of the cars as it passed; a look of excitement was on the kid's freckled face.

The church got more ominous with each step and dread poured into every crevice of Joe's mind. He wasn't sure if the preacher had any more tricks up his sleeve, but at this point, Joe couldn't rule out the possibility that Plunkett would shoot him the moment he saw him.

Wishing he had a mind to find the gun before they left the house, Joe thought through what he would do when they got to the church. He knew Plunkett would be expecting them, eventually, so the idea of trying to sneak up on the church made no sense. Never one for planning, Joe decided that he would just walk through the front door and figure it out from there.

Lost in thought about what he was walking into, Joe was startled when he realized that he was standing at the feet of the steps leading up to the church. The pristine white building towered ominously above him. He feared the steeple would come crashing down upon him when he set foot inside, a thought that he hadn't considered up until this point.

If he was evil and this was a holy place, could he even enter it?

Having conjured forth a horde of fox-devils, would he burst into flames the moment he breached the doors of the church? Did he now carry the mark of Cain or the number of the beast? In a world where fox-devils could be summoned by a book found in the local library, which was first introduced to him by a cartoon, Joe felt it wasn't a long shot that God might even be real. He didn't really care, and he doubted it would smite him or set him ablaze, as it hadn't yet.

Breathing in one final smell of morning air, Joe cracked his knuckles and started up the steps to the church. When he looked back to see if the fox-devils were following him, or if this was hallowed, untouchable ground that they could not enter, Joe was shocked that they were no longer with him. Once again, they had vanished, leaving only faint-red paw prints where they had been. Not sure if this was part of a plan they had, if they were afraid of getting shot again, or if they really couldn't cross into God's house, Joe reluctantly forged on without them, cursing the whole time.

The heavy wooden doors cried out loudly as Joe pushed them open, the sound echoing through the vacant church. One foot in front of the other and he was inside, a little disappointed that he hadn't burst into flames or been smitten by a bolt of lightning from the heavens. He paused in anticipation of something happening, but nothing ever came.

The chapel was dimly lit by sunlight coming through the stained-glass windows on either side of the long room. There were no lights, there was no movement. Pensively, Joe walked down the middle aisle, like a bride marching to meet her fate. He was about halfway to the altar when Plunkett came out from a side-door on the small stage. He was holding a gun in one hand and a bible in the other as he walked silently to the pulpit. He spoke as he stopped at the dark wood lectern.

"I have failed many times before, but I will not fail you now, son. The evil that is within you can be extinguished and cast out. All you have to do is fight against it and come back into the loving arms of God," his voice trembled with every word.

Joe fought back tears, "You killed my fucking mom, asshole! You ruined my goddamn family. Fuck you and your god. I want to know what the fuck you did to my brother before I tear your eyes from your head."

"Silence, wretched demon! Let the boy go, in the name of Christ, I command that you set him free of your demonic chains."

"You killed my goddamn mom and ruined my fucking family, you fucking monster," the tears broke as Joe yelled. "What the fuck did you do to my fucking brother? There's nothing you can do and nowhere you can go. I will find you. We will find you."

"And you killed your own father, guided by the occult hand of Satan himself. Your brother was already headed toward the fiery gates of hell; there was nothing I could do for him.

"I was too weak..."

With that, the fox-devils made their appearance, standing throughout the sanctuary of the church, their black eyes focused on Plunkett.

"In the name of the most high God, I command you demons out of this holy place. You are not welcome here and I rebuke you in the name of Jesus."

The pack stood unswayed.

Without another word, Plunkett lifted the revolver, aiming it at Joe, and pulled the trigger.

Before Joe had a chance to react, a shot filled the church like a hymnal chorus. The bullet ripped into his chest and pierced his lung. A marionette with its strings clipped, he fell to the floor, unable to breathe. The world went grey, as he struggled to make sense of what had just happened. His heart pounded in his ears like a jack-hammer and his hands were slick with blood gushing from his chest. All he could think was, "It wasn't supposed to end like this," as the grey world got darker and more distant. Joe saw a flurry of movement on the chapel stage, blurred by tears and waning focus. The sanctuary filled with several more gunshots. Right before he felt himself slip away completely, he heard agonizing screams echoing through the church.

The priest's final sermon.

✝

A new warmth filled Joe's cold body as he started to regain consciousness. Opening his eyes, he was surrounded by the fox-devils; the smallest of them was standing on his chest. Its wounds and scars getting more tattered as it stared down at him with deep, black eyes. A patch of ivory bone got bigger on its snout, exposing red gums and shimmering teeth.

Joe's strength was returning. He felt better with every passing moment. Rising up, reborn of tooth and claw, he felt at one with the pack; united in blood and fur. Looking down, he watched the spent bullet push out of his healing skin and clang to the wooden floor below.

The foxes began their low, single-voiced song and Joe joined them, his own voice now soaring irregularly above theirs, causing an unnatural harmony. Inside, the could feel the full merging of the bright white nothing and the great black unknown. He and the foxes had fully become one.

And as quickly as that, they were gone.

But he could still feel them, inside. He could hear their chatter and knew that now they'd never leave.

Plunkett's corpse was a mess. Scarcely a body at all, more of an assorted pile of body parts, jelly, and a mutilated head. The fox-devils had plucked both of his eyes out, ripped off his ears, and toren out his tongue. Joe felt no pity, no anger, only silent satisfaction.

Staring into the hollowed-out eyes of the reverend, Joe let the black flames rise inside his soul. He thought about his family, his brother, his mother, his father. He remembered what life was like before Stan left; before existence was nothing but a grey and lifeless chore. Joe thought about color and life.

Near his left shoulder, a small black flame floated in the air.

As he walked out of the church, Joe thought about that flame dancing around the chapel, kissing every piece of fabric and wood that it could. He thought about that flame growing and consuming Plunkett, about the way Plunkett had consumed so much of Joe's life. He thought about that flame overtaking the sanctuary, consuming the entire structure, and bringing the steeple down.

With smoke and black-burning heat following behind him, Joe thought about asking the black flame to consume everything.

✝

AFTERWORD

The road to making *Sabbath of the Fox-Devils* a reality was quite a bizarre one. Initially, I started this project in one of Garrett Cook's amazing novella workshops. This was early 2017, though the concept for the book had been rattling around in my brain for years, with several false-starts.

While the book is certainly a love-letter to 80s small-creature horror, one of my all-time favorite micro-genres, it is also an exploration of my own experiences growing up in a rather extreme branch of the Pentecostal church. Tapping that vein was a challenging task.

But with the help of Garrett and the other workshop attendees, I was able to push into the murky, uncomfortable waters of what I wanted to explore. For that, I owe them all my deepest thanks.

I was slowly chipping away at the book when my life came to a grinding and terrible halt in August of 2017 when my wife, Mo, died unexpectedly of an aortic aneurysm.

During that time, it's not an exaggeration to say that writing kept me alive. The bulk of that output became my debut collection, *To Wallow in Ash & Other Sorrows*. As the time passed and I slowly adapted to my horrible new 'normal,' the novella kept creeping into the back of my mind.

Mo was my biggest fan and supporter. She was always there to help me and was the first person to read everything I finished. I have great memories of the two of us sitting on our couch, listening to music while I wrote and she drew her tattoos for the next day. Together but in our own creative worlds. I fucking miss that. I fucking miss her.

Fox-Devils was something that she had heard me talk about at great length, as I worked out the story beats and how to get from a-to-b. In the wake of her passing, I knew I couldn't let it sit unfinished. I knew she would want me to make it happen. Even in death, I can still feel her rooting for me.

But the timing was wrong for the first couple of years. I had other stories I *needed* to be writing. While there is a component of grief within, at it's core *Fox-Devils* isn't about grief; and I didn't want to inject what I was going through into the story I had already built. So I poured my sorrows elsewhere until I was ready to process something else.

In 2019 I found the energy and focus, following the publication of *To Wallow in Ash & Other Sorrows*. And while there is a very personal emotional core to this book, it is an entirely different beast than those grief-based stories. In a word, this one is a lot more fun. I will return to the realm of sorrow with my next book, but it was important to me that this finally see the light of day; that I finally move past it and onto other projects.

Like all books, this is for Mo, who I will never stop loving, despite the unbreakable boundaries between us. Wherever she is or isn't, I know she'd be proud.

✝

ACKNOWLEDGMENTS

This book wouldn't be possible without the support of Jes, thank you so much for all your flexibility and encouragement. I appreciate it to the ends of the earth.

A massive amount of gratitude is due to Garrett Cook, who helped me begin this journey in his workshop all those years ago.

My weird writer family is also largely to blame. Huge hugs and eternal thanks to Jo Quenell, Brendan Vidito, Charles Austin Muir, and Mark Zirbel for all the help, guidance, and laughter.

Lucas Mangum, Katy Michelle Quinn, and Ryan Harding are some of the kindest, most amazing people ever and I owe them more than I could ever give.

Emma Alice Johnson has always been one of my biggest supporters and friends. I truly wouldn't be here without her.

Danger Slater, who was so encouraging and helpful when this book was still in its infancy even though we hadn't known each other for very long.

Leo X. Robertson, Madeleine Swann, S.C. Burke, Leza Cantoral, Christoph Paul, Frank Edler, Sam Reeve, Ira Rat, Ben Fitts, Andrew Wayne Adams, Gwendolyn Kiste, Nick Day, Chris Kelso, Tiffany Scandal, Robert S. Wilson, John Wayne Communale, Tim Murr, Austin James, and tons of other amazing writers. Support these people. Buy their books. You won't regret it.

Michael Bukowski and Don Nobel, both of whom I am lucky enough to have worked with on several books. Thank you for dealing with my hyper-specific requests and absurd ideas. You both made this thing beautiful.

Extra-special thanks to my dad and sister, who have been massively supportive of my writing career. Thank you!

The other member of Ash Eater, for always being the best folks.

The list is endless, to all my friends and family, thank you! Sorry I can't name you all.

Don't forget to kiss the goat.

ABOUT THE AUTHOR

The owner of Weirdpunk Books, Sam Richard is also the co-editor of the Splatterpunk Award nominated *The New Flesh: A Literary Tribute to David Cronenberg* and editor of *Zombie Punks Fuck Off*. 2019 saw the release of his debut collection, *To Wallow in Ash & Other Sorrows*, and his short fiction has appeared in *LAZERMALL, Strange Stories of the Sea, Breaking Bizarro*, and many other anthologies and publications. Widowed in 2017, he slowly rots in Minneapolis, MN with his dog Nero. He dreams of writing a musical-theater adaptation of Bataille's *Story of the Eye*. *Sabbath of the Fox-Devils* is his first novella.

Also By Weirdpunk Books

The Mud Ballad - Jo Quenell

NEVER BE ALONE AGAIN

In a dying railroad town, a conjoined twin wallows in purgatory for the murder of his brother. A disgraced surgeon goes to desperate ends to reconnect with his lost love. When redemption comes with a dash of black magic, the two enter a world of talking corpses, flesh-eating hogs, rude mimes, and ritualistic violence.

"Jo Quenell's debut novella explores both regret and connection in the weirdest and wildest ways possible. Good times!"

— DANGER SLATER, AUTHOR OF THE WONDERLAND AWARD WINNING *I WILL ROT WITHOUT YOU*

The New Flesh: A Literary Tribute to David Cronenberg -
Edited by Sam Richard and Brendan Vidito

Videodrome. Scanners. The Brood. Crash. The Fly. The films of
David Cronenberg have haunted and inspired generations.
His name has become synonymous with the body horror
subgenere and the term "Cronenbergian" has been used to
describe the stark, grotesque, and elusive quality of his work.
These eighteen stories bring his themes and ideas into the
present, throbbing with unnatural life.

A Splatterpunk Awards nominee for Best Anthology, The
New Flesh features stories by Brain Evenson, Gwendolyn
Kiste, Cody Goodfellow, Katy Michelle Quinn, Ryan
Harding, and more. Plus an introduction by the legendary
Kathe Koja!

Zombie Punks Fuck Off - Edited by Sam Richard

(Co-published with CLASH Books)

We've been hearing forever that punk is dead. And zombie stories are even deader. *Zombie Punks Fuck Off* is here to show that is bullshit. This anthology is loaded with 14 stories of gnawing teeth, shredded entrails, rotting masses, punk as fuck fury, post-punk weirdness, and beautiful decay.

Featuring stories by Danger Slater, Emma Alice Johnson, David W. Barbee, Carmilla Voiez, Asher Ellis, and more.

CPSIA information can be obtained
at www.ICGtesting.com
Printed in the USA
LVHW090851150721
692729LV00002B/98